RUSKIN BOND

Funny Side Up

Published by
Rupa Publications India Pvt. Ltd 2006
7/16, Ansari Road, Daryaganj
New Delhi 110002

Sales centres:
Bengaluru Chennai
Hyderabad Jaipur Kathmandu
Kolkata Mumbai Prayagraj

Copyright © Ruskin Bond 2006

This is a work of fiction. Names, characters, places and incidents are either the product of the author's imagination or are used fictitiously and any resemblance to any actual person, living or dead, events or locales is entirely coincidental.

All rights reserved.
No part of this publication may be reproduced, transmitted, or stored in a retrieval system, in any form or by any means, electronic, mechanical, photocopying, recording or otherwise, without the prior permission of the publisher.

P-ISBN: 978-81-291-0828-9
E-ISBN: 978-81-291-2311-4

Twenty-third impression 2025

30 29 28 27 26 25 24 23

The moral right of the author has been asserted.

Printed in India

This book is sold subject to the condition that it shall not, by way of trade or otherwise, be lent, resold, hired out, or otherwise circulated, without the publisher's prior consent, in any form of binding or cover other than that in which it is published.

Funny Side Up

Ruskin Bond has been writing for over sixty years, and now has over 120 titles in print—novels, collections of short stories, poetry, essays, anthologies and books for children. His first novel, *The Room on the Roof*, received the prestigious John Llewellyn Rhys Prize in 1957. He has also received the Padma Shri (1999), the Padma Bhushan (2014) and two awards from Sahitya Akademi—one for his short stories and another for his writings for children. In 2012, the Delhi government gave him its Lifetime Achievement Award.

Born in 1934, Ruskin Bond grew up in Jamnagar, Shimla, New Delhi and Dehradun. Apart from three years in the UK, he has spent all his life in India, and now lives in Mussoorie with his adopted family.

By the same author:

Angry River
A Little Night Music
A Long Walk for Bina
Hanuman to the Rescue
Ghost Stories from the Raj
Strange Men, Strange Places
The India I Love
Tales and Legends from India
The Blue Umbrella
Ruskin Bond's Children's Omnibus
The Ruskin Bond Omnibus-I
The Ruskin Bond Omnibus-II
The Ruskin Bond Omnibus-III
Rupa Book of Great Animal Stories
The Rupa Book of True Tales of Mystery and Adventure
The Rupa Book of Ruskin Bond's Himalayan Tales
The Rupa Book of Great Suspense Stories
The Rupa Laughter Omnibus
The Rupa Book of Scary Stories
The Rupa Book of Haunted Houses
The Rupa Book of Travellers' Tales
The Rupa Book of Great Crime Stories
The Rupa Book of Nightmare Tales
The Rupa Book of Shikar Stories
The Rupa Book of Love Stories
The Rupa Book of Wicked Stories
The Rupa Book of Heartwarming Stories
The Rupa Book of Thrills and Spills

A little nonsense now and then,

is relished by the wisest men.

CONTENTS

Introduction	ix
Belting around Mumbai	1
Monkey on the Roof	5
And in the Loo	12
And at the Bank	20
If Mice Could Row	28
In Search of Sweet-peas	30
The Regimental Myna	38
Monkey Trouble	44
Frogs in the Fountain	57
On Foot with Faith	64
The Zigzag Walk	73

A Bicycle Ride with Uncle Ken	77
At Sea with Uncle Ken	84
Travels with my Bank Manager	92
Granny's Tree-Climbing	102
My Failed Omelettes—and other Disasters	105
A Long Story	108
George and Ranji	111
Cricket—Field Placings	115
Whatever Happened to Romance?	116
In Praise of Older Women	124
Who Kissed me in the Dark?	135
A Frog Screams	142
All you Need Is Paper	144
Song for a Beetle in a Goldfish Bowl	151
Odds and Ends	153

INTRODUCTION

The monkey population is definitely on the increase, and I wouldn't be surprised if one day it exceeds the human population. Of course, the way things are going, a time may come when we won't be able to distinguish between monkeys and humans. Monkeys are becoming more human, while humans are becoming more like monkeys.

Summer nights I leave my window open, and early this morning a member of the Rhesus tribe entered stealthily, picked up my notebook, and made a quick exit. I was in time to see him on a neighbouring roof, trying to chew up the notebook. Finding it unappetising, he proceeded to tear it to shreds and scatter the pieces over the hillside.

In this way I lost one chapter of my book, and the reader will have to put up with twenty-six chapters instead of twenty-seven.

Not that the missing chapter was a great loss to literature. It dealt chiefly with my neighbour's pigeons, who are apt to fly in at my window from time to time, and leave their droppings on my desk. I have nothing against pigeons—they gave me the title for a story once—but Professor Saili informs me that Bird Flu is spread through the droppings of various domesticated birds such as ducks, geese, pigeons and poultry. A fowl subject, but one to be heeded. So now I shoo the pigeons away, where once I welcomed them. They must take their droppings to the nearest statue, clocktower, or old police station.

Talking of birds, I must mention the hill myna who occasionally perches on the ledge below my window. Hill mynas are great mimics, and my visitor often imitates the calls of other birds and various human sounds. An elderly gentleman who lives next door had been away for a fortnight. He was given to much early morning coughing, throat clearing, and hawking. I thought he had returned when I woke up to the sound of his usual coughing and spluttering. Getting up and looking out, I saw that his door was still locked. But perched on the railing was the myna, giving a perfect imitation of the old gentleman's early morning throat-clearing exercise. When he does return he will find he has a competitor.

Birds can do some funny things. My toothbrushes kept disappearing, and I had no idea why, until one day I saw a smart black jungle crow strutting along the parapet wall with my toothbrush held in his beak. Later we found he had made quite a collection of them in a space between the ceiling and the roof. No wonder toothbrush sales have been going up.

Of course people are funnier than animals, and most of the funny stories in this book are about people: Uncle Ken,

Aunt Mabel, my nature-loving bank manager, girls I can't forget, old flames, young flames, and most of all your befuddled author, to whom funny things keep happening all the time. And there's seven-year-old Gautam, who brings a little sanity to the proceedings.

'Why do you write books?' he asked me the other day. 'Doesn't your hand get tired?'

'After some time,' I said. 'But I write books in order to make a living.'

'Isn't there anything else you can do?'

I thought hard for a minute. There didn't seem to be much else I could do. Then I brightened up.

'I can boil an egg,' I said.

Gautam clapped his hands. 'Oh, good! We can sell boiled eggs on the Mall, opposite Cambridge Bookshop. You won't have to write books anymore.'

'But I like writing,' I protested. 'And besides, we won't make much money selling eggs. There's too much competition.'

'And what about writers? Aren't there too many?'

'Yes, but they are all serious writers. I'm just a funny writer. They make omelettes. I make scrambled eggs.'

'What's a scrambled egg?'

'What you eat every morning—anda-ka-bhuji?'

'Oh, I like it that way. Don't make serious omelettes, Dada. Be a scrambled writer.' He gave me a big hug and ran off, shouting, 'Dada-ka-bhuji!'

1

BELTING AROUND MUMBAI

I have lived to see Bombay become Mumbai, Calcutta become Kolkata, and Madras become Chennai. Times change, names change, and if Bond becomes Bonda I won't object. Place-names may alter but people don't, and in Mumbai I found that people were as friendly and good-natured as ever; perhaps even more than when I was last there twenty-five years ago.

On that occasion I had travelled the Doon Express, a slow passenger train that stopped at every small station in at least five states, taking two days and two nights from Dehradun to Bombay. It had been a fairly uneventful journey, except for an incident in the small hours when we stopped at Baroda and a hand slipped through my open window, crept under my pillow, found nothing of value except my spectacles, and decided to take them anyway, leaving me to grope half-blind around Bombay until another pair could be made.

Now I carry three pairs of spectacles: one for reading, one for looking at people, and one for looking far out to sea.

On the Kingfisher flight to Mumbai, I used the second pair, as I like looking at people, especially attractive air hostesses. I found they were looking at me too, but that was because I'd caught my belt (my trouser belt, not my seat-belt) in a fellow-passenger's luggage strap and was proceeding to drag both him and his travel-bag down the aisle. We were diplomatically separated by the aforesaid air hostesses who then guided me to my seat without further mishap.

This reminded me of the occasion many years ago when I auditioned for a role in a Tarzan film.

'Who do you wish to play?' asked the casting director.

'Tarzan, of course,' I said.

He gave me a long hard look. 'Can you swing from one tree to another?' he asked.

'Easily,' I said. 'I can even swing from a chandelier.' And I proceeded to do so, wrecking the hall they sat in, in the process. They begged me to stop.

'Thank you, Mr Bond, you have made your point. But we don't think you have the figure for the part of Tarzan. Would you like to take the part of the missionary who is being cooked to a crisp by a bunch of cannibals? Tarzan will come to your rescue.'

I declined the role with dignity.

And now I was in Mumbai, not to audition for a film, but to inaugurate the Rupa Book Festival. For old time's sake, I arrived at the venue in a horse-drawn carriage. Alighting, my recalcitrant belt-buckle got entangled with the horse's harness and I almost dragged the entire contraption into the Bajaj exhibition hall.

However, the evening's entertainment went off without a hitch. Gulzar read from Ghalib, Tom Alter read from Gulzar, Mandira Bedi read from Nandita Puri, and everyone read madly from each other, and I sat quietly in a corner to keep my belt out of further entanglements.

The next day I was taken on a tour of the city by a *Hindustan Times* journalist and a photographer. They asked me to pose on the steps of the Asiatic Society's Library, an imposing colonial edifice. While I stood there being photographed, a group of teenagers walked past and I overheard one of them remark: 'Yeh naya model hain.'

I took it as a compliment. At least they didn't call me a purana model. Perhaps there's still a chance to get that Tarzan role. If not Tarzan, then his grandfather.

The same journalist and photographer took me to a market where you could buy anything from books to bras. They thrust a thousand-rupee note into my willing hands and told me I could buy anything I liked, while they took pictures.

'Can I keep the money?' I asked.

'No, you have to spend it.'

So I bought two ladies handbags and two pairs of ladies slippers.

'For your girlfriends?' asked the journalist.

'No,' I said, 'for their mothers.'

Back at the festival hall, I was presented with a beautiful sky-blue T-shirt by a charming lady who wishes to remain anonymous. I wore it the next morning when I was leaving Mumbai.

At the airport, one of the Kingfisher staff complimented me on my dress sense; the first time anyone has done so.

'Your blue shirt matches your eyes,' she said.

After that, I shall definitely fly Kingfisher again.

2

MONKEY ON THE ROOF

1

Quite often, I'm up with the lark—more often, with the sound of monkeys jumping on my tin roof. I've often wondered why hill-station houses must have these rusty red tin roofs, apart from an understandable human desire to make them look like battered old biscuit tins. Well, now I know. They are there for the benefit of monkeys, langurs, field-rats, cats, crows, mynas, spiders and scorpions.

I don't mind the spiders—they seem harmless enough. The scorpions are evil-looking but sluggish—unlike the dashing red scorpions of the Rajasthan desert. The other day I found a scorpion enjoying a nap on my pillow. I like to have my pillow to myself, so I tipped the slumbering creature out of the window and returned to my afternoon siesta. I do not take the lives of fellow creatures if I can help it. Cats are not so squeamish. At night they get between the tin roof and the wooden ceiling and create havoc among the rats and mice who dwell there. And early morning, if I leave a window open, the monkeys will finish anything they find on the breakfast table.

In spite of occasional rude awakenings, I enjoy sleeping late, especially on winter mornings when the sun struggles to penetrate banks of cloud or mist or drizzle. The bed is one of my favourite places. And even if I am wide awake, I can lie there under the blanket and razai and enjoy the view without rising. The window in front of me looks out on the clouds or the clear sky; the window beside it gives me a view of upper Landour and the houses on the slopes; and the far window looks out on a thicket of oak trees. And if I sit up in bed, I can see the road and some of the people on it.

But to start with my bed, for that's where the day begins and ends. There's something to be said for beds. After all, we spend roughly half our lives stretched out upon them. The amount of time spent in sleep varies from one individual to another.

'Five hours sleepeth a traveller, seven a scholar, eight a merchant, and eleven every knave.'

So goes an old proverb, and there is much truth in proverbs. I must fall somewhere between merchant and knave. There are times when I like to rise early and times when I enjoy sleeping late. If I fall asleep before midnight, I will rise early.

One hour's sleep before midnight is worth two after. When the moon is up, the night has its magic; but at two or three in the morning there is very little to offer, because by ten even cats, bats and field-rats are asleep. In summer, bird-song starts at dawn, somewhere between four and five o'clock and that's a good time to be up and about, exercising mind or body.

The other morning I was up at five; wrote a couple of pages, opened my window and swallowed a portion of cloud; closed it, conscience clear, and returned to bed where presently a cup of tea materialised, prepared by Beena or Dolly or some other member of the family. But for that morning cup of tea, would I have survived all these years? Without it, the mornings would be one long, endless wasteland. Without it, I would not get up. I would refuse breakfast, lunch and dinner, and waste away. Looking back upon my life from the vantage point of seventy years, I cannot remember a time when I was deprived of that morning cup of tea. Except for when I was in boarding school. Now you know why I ran away.

Getting up and making my own tea is no fun either. It has to be brought to me by some gentle soul—man, woman or child—who has got up before everyone else in order to ensure that I get up too.

The best tea I've ever drunk was made by an ex-convict who worked for my landlady in Dehradun, many years ago. He told me that while he was in jail he was assigned to the task of making the warden's tea. It was appreciated so much that they wouldn't let him go even after he'd served his sentence. How, then, did he gain his freedom? Well, my landlady was the wife of the jail superintendent. So you see how well the system worked!

For a while in London, I had a Jewish landlady who brought me my breakfast on a tray. I don't know if such civilised courtesies still exist. Back in the 1950s, English food was not very exciting; it had yet to be enriched by Indian curries and Chinese noodles. But breakfasts were always good—far superior to the skimpy fare served out by the French. Bacon and eggs, marmalade on toast, occasionally a kipper, a sausage, a slice of ham, grapefruit...what more could anyone ask for at the start of a busy day? And even now, when the days aren't quite so busy, I might skip lunch or dinner but I'll breakfast well.

So finally I'm out of bed and enjoying my breakfast. The children have gone to school and silence has descended on the house. A day in the life of Ruskin Bond is about to commence. I am at liberty to write a poem or a story or fill these pages with inconsequential thoughts. But first I must get dressed.

I am not fond of clothes, but I wouldn't care to start the day's work without at least wearing a clean shirt. When I was a struggling young writer, I did not possess more than two shirts at one time, but I would wash one every night in the hope that it would be dry by morning. Even today, I don't have a large wardrobe. It isn't possible, not with all these monkeys around. If you see a large red monkey wearing a blue and yellow check bush-shirt, please try and retrieve it for me; it's my favourite shirt. Putting clothes out on the roof to dry is fairly common practice in hill-stations, but not to be recommended. Only the other day, when a strong wind came up from the east, I saw my pyjamas floating away downhill to end up entangled in the branches of an oak tree. Fortunately the milkman's son, who is good at climbing oak trees, rescued them for me. The milkman's son does not pass his exams, but as long as he can climb trees, he'll be a success in life. All of us need just one good accomplishment in order to get by. Obviously he can't spend the rest of his life climbing trees, but it's the agility and enterprise involved in the act that will make him a survivor.

Enough of bed and breakfast and getting ready for the long morning's journey into day. When does this ageing writer sit down to write? Or does he simply dictate to a secretary or into a machine of some kind? Well, I wish that was the case, because I'm a lazy sort of writer, better in bed than out of it. Unfortunately, I get tongue-tied when I try to tell a story, make a speech, or conduct something as simple as a telephone or cell phone conversation.

Recently Dolly made me buy a mobile phone; it would make me more efficient and up-to-date, she said. I tried making a call, and when nothing happened, she said, 'Dada, you're holding it upside down!' I got it the right way up and tried again, and when nothing happened, she said, 'Not here. You have to go to the window.'

I dutifully walked over and tried again. No luck. 'Open the window,' ordered Dolly. I opened the window. Just a crackle on the cell phone. 'Now look out of the window!' I looked out, and there were all these schoolgirls gazing up at me, wondering why I was staring down at them. 'Good morning girls,' I called out, and gave them a friendly wave. 'No girls here,' said a gruff voice on the cell phone. 'This is your local thana.'

I gave the mobile to Dolly. She has no difficulty in getting through to her friends, or hearing from them. I'm no good at these things, except to pay the bill.

I'm strictly a man of the written word. Give me pen and paper and I manage to get something down, even if it's only for my own amusement. An elderly reader once remarked, 'How do you manage to write so much about nothing?' to which I could only reply: 'Well, it's better than writing nothing about everything!'

That small red ant walking across my desk may mean nothing to the world at large, but to me it represents the world at large. It represents industry, single-mindedness, intricacy of design, the perfection of nature, the miracle of creation. So much so, that it inspires me to poetic composition:

You stride through the wasteland of my desk,
Pressing on over books and papers,
Down the wall and across the floor—
Small red ant, now crossing a sea of raindrops
At my open door.
Your destiny, your task
To carry home
That heavy sunflower seed,

Waving it like a banner
Of victory!

Nothing is insignificant; nothing is without consequence in the intricate web of life.

3

AND IN THE LOO

I am fairly tolerant about these monkeys doing the bhangra on my roof, but I do resent it when they start invading my rooms. Not so long ago, I opened the bathroom door to find a very large Rhesus monkey sitting on the potty. He wasn't actually using the potty—monkeys prefer parapet walls—but he had obviously found it a comfortable place to sit, and he showed no signs of vacating the throne when politely requested to do so. Bullies seldom do. So I had to give him a fright by slamming the door as loudly as I could, and he took off through the open window and found his cousins on the hillside.

On another occasion, a female of the species sat on my desk, lifted the telephone receiver and appeared to be making an STD call to some distant relative. Some ladies are apt to linger long over their calls, and I hated to interrupt, but I was anxious to get in touch with my publisher, who took priority; so I pushed her off my desk with a feather-duster. She was so resentful of this intrusion that she made off with my telephone directory and tore it to shreds, scattering pages along the road. As this was something that I had wanted to do for a long time, I could not help admiring her audacity.

The kitchen area of our flat is closely guarded, as I resent sharing my breakfast with creatures great and small. But the other day a wily crow flew in and made off with my boiled egg. I know crows are fond of eggs—other birds' eggs that is—but I did not know that they like them boiled. Anyway, this egg was still piping hot, and the crow had to drop it on the road, where it was seized upon by one of the stray dogs who police this end of the road.

Barking furiously, the dogs run after the monkeys, who simply leap onto the nearest tree or rooftop and proceed to throw insults at the frustrated pack. The dogs never succeed in catching anything except their own kind. Canine intruders from another area are readily attacked and driven away.

Having dressed, breakfasted and written the morning's two or three pages (early morning is the best time to do this), I am free to walk up the road to the bank or post office or tea shop at the top of the hill. If it's springtime, I shall look out for wild flowers. If it's monsoon time; I shall look out for leeches.

Well, it's monsoon time, and we haven't seen the sun for a couple of weeks. Clouds envelop the hills, and a light shower is falling. I have unfurled my bright yellow umbrella, as a gesture of defiance. At least it provides some contrast to the grey sky and the dark green of the hillside. You cannot see the snows or even the next mountain.

There's no one else on the road today, only a few intrepid tourists from Amritsar. I overhead one robust Punjabi complain to his guide: 'You've brought us all the way to the top of this forsaken mountain, and what have you shown us? The kabristan!'

True, the old British graves are all that one can see through the fog. Some of the tombstones have been standing there for close on two centuries. The old abandoned parsonage next door to the cemetery is now the home of Victor Banerjee, the celebrated actor. He enjoys living next door to the graveyard, and one night he defied me to walk home alone past the graves. I am not a superstitious person but I did feel rather uneasy as those old graves loomed up through the mist. I was startled by the cry of a night-bird emanating from behind one of the tombstones. Then a weird, blood-chilling cry rose from a clump of bushes. It was Victor, trying to frighten me—or possibly practicing for his next role as Dracula. I was about to break into a run when a large dog—one of our strays—appeared beside me and accompanied me home. On a dark and scary night, even a half-starved mongrel is welcome company.

By day, the road holds no terrors. But there are other hazards. On the road near Char Duskan, several small boys are kicking a football around. The ball rolls temptingly towards me. Remembering my football skills of fifty or more years ago, I cannot resist the temptation to put boot to ball. I give it a mighty kick. The ball sails away, the children applaud, I am left hopping about on the road in agony, I had quite forgotten my gout!

I'm glad I stuck to writing instead of taking up professional football. At seventy I can still write without inflicting damage on myself.

When I am feeling good, and have the road to myself, I do occasionally break into song. This is the only opportunity I have to sing. Otherwise my musical abilities turn friends into foes.

I am not permitted to sing in the homes of my friends. If I am being driven about in their cars, I am told to remain silent unless we veer off the road or hit an oncoming vehicle. Even at home, the sound of my music causes the girls to drop dishes and the children to find an excuse to stop doing their homework.

'Dada is ill again,' says Gautam, when all I am trying to do is emulate Caruso singing *Che Gelida Manina* (Your Tiny Hand is Frozen) from *La Bohéme*. Our tiny hands do freeze up here in the winter, and there's nothing like an operatic aria to get the blood circulating freely. Of course Caruso was a tenor, but I can also sing baritone like Domingo or Nelson

Eddy and bass like Chaliapin the great Russian singer. Sometimes I combine all three voices—tenor, baritone, bass—and that's when the window glass shatters and cars come to a screeching halt.

It was a boyhood ambition to be an opera star, but I'm afraid I never made it beyond the school choir. Our music teacher did not appreciate the wide range of my voice.

'Too loud!' she would screech. 'Too flat!'

'Caruso sings in A-flat,' I replied.

'You sound like a warbling frog,' she snapped.

'And you look like one,' I responded.

And that was the end of my brief appearance in cassock and surplice.

But when I'm on the open road—especially when it's raining and I have the road to myself—I am free to sing as loud and as flat as I like, and if flat tyres on passing cars are the result, it's the fault of the tyres and not my singing.

So here we go:

> 'When you are down and out,
> Lift up your head and shout—
> It's going to be a great day!'

There's nothing like a spirited song to raise the flagging spirit. Whenever I feel down and out—and that's often enough—I recall some old favourite and share it with the trees, the birds, and even those pesky monkeys.

'Just like a sunflower
After a summer shower
My inspiration is you!'
Sloppy, sentimental stuff, but it works.

And there's always the likelihood of a little romance around the corner.

'Some enchanted evening
You will see a stranger
Across a crowded room...'

Actually, I prefer the winding road to a crowded room. Romantic encounters are more likely when there are not too many people around. Such as the other day, when I had unfurled my new umbrella and was sauntering up the road, singing my favourite rain song, *Singing in the Rain*.

I had gone some distance when I noticed a young lady struggling up the road a little way ahead of me. My glasses were wet and misty, but I was determined to share my umbrella with any damsel in distress. So, huffing and puffing, I caught up with her.

'Do share my umbrella,' I offered.

No, she wasn't sweet twenty-one, as I'd hoped. She was nearer eighty. But she was munching on a bhutta, so her teeth were in good order. She took the umbrella from me and munched on ahead, leaving me to get drenched. A retired headmistress, as I discovered later!

She returned the umbrella when we got to Char Dukan, but in future I shall make a frontal approach before making any gallant overtures on the road. Those crowded rooms are safer.

Monsoon time, and umbrellas are taken out and frequently lost. I lost three last year. One was borrowed, and as you know, borrowed books and umbrellas are seldom returned. By some mysterious process they become the permanent property of the borrower. Another disappeared while I was cashing a cheque in the bank. And the third was wrecked in the following fashion.

Coming down from Char Dukan, I found two hefty boys engaged in furious combat in the middle of the road. One was a kick-boxer, the other a kung-fu exponent. Afraid that one of them would be badly hurt, I decided to intervene, and called out, 'Come on boys, break it up!' I thrust my umbrella between them in a bid to end the fracas. My umbrella received a mighty kick, and went sailing across the road and over the parapet. The boys stopped fighting in order to laugh at my discomfiture. One of them retrieved my umbrella, minus its handle.

In a way, I'd been successful as a peacemaker—certainly more successful than the United Nations—although at some cost to my personal property. Well, we peacemakers must be prepared to put up with a little inconvenience.

I'm a great believer in the Law of Compensation (as propounded by Emerson in his famous essay)—that what we do, good or bad, is returned in full measure in this life rather than in the hereafter.

Not long after the incident just described, there was my old friend Vipin Buckshey standing on the threshold with a seasonal gift—a beautiful blue umbrella!

He did not know about the street-fighter, but had read my story *The Blue Umbrella*—a simple tale about greed being overcome by generosity—and had bought me a blue umbrella in appreciation. I shall be careful not to lose it.

4

AND AT THE BANK

Yes, those monkeys are at the bank too. They are there before it opens, doing their best to damage the roof; and they are there when it closes, tearing up the geraniums so lovingly planted by the manager.

I am also there when it opens, having, as usual, run short over the weekend, with the result that all I have in my pocket is a damaged fifty rupee note which I have attempted to repair with Sellotape.

The bank opens promptly at ten a.m. Unfortunately, it doesn't have any money. No, it has not collapsed like the old Mansaram Bank, for which Ganesh Saili still has his father's chequebook showing a balance of three hundred rupees in 1957; the taxi with the cash (which comes from the main branch) has been caught in a traffic jam due to an unprecedented influx of tourists. This happens occasionally, as there are only two ways in and out of Mussoorie and only one way to Char Dukan.

Anyway, I pass the time by having a cup of tea with the manager and discussing the latest cricket test match with the cashier.

He is of the opinion that the result of a match depends on who wins the toss, while I maintain that the game is won by the team that has slept better the night before.

The cash arrives safely and I emerge into the sunshine to be met by several small boys who demand money for a cricket ball. I part with a new fifty rupee note (the old one having been obligingly changed by the cashier) and then run into several members of Tom Alter's cricket team, who insist that I join their Invitation XI in a game against the Dhobi Ghat Team, about to be played up at Chey-Tanki flat. (This was before the area got fenced off by the Defence establishment as cricket balls kept sailing into their offices and smashing their computers.)

Forgetting my age, but remembering my great days as a twelfth man for the Doon Heroes, I consented on condition that a substitute would field in my place. (No longer would I be a twelfth man.)

Well, the Dhobi Ghat Team put up a good score, and Tom's Invitation XI was trailing by some sixty or seventy runs, when I came in to bat at number seven. Tom was at the other end, holding the innings together.

The bowler (who ran a dry-cleaner's in town) was a real speedster, and his first ball caught me in the midriff. I am well padded there (by nature) but I resolved not to use that dry-cleaner's shop again. The second ball took the edge of my bat and sped away for four.

'Well played, Ruskin!' called Tom encouragingly, and I resolved to write a part for him in my next story.

I tapped the third ball into the covers and set off for a run, completely forgetting that I hadn't taken a run in fifty years. Still, I got to the other end, gasping for breath and trembling in the legs. Next, Tom tapped the ball away and called me for a run! There was no way I was going to join the brave souls sleeping in Jogger's Park (the name for the Landour cemetery), so I held up my hand and remained rooted to the crease. Tom was half-way down the pitch when the ball hit his stumps and he was run out. The look he gave me as he marched back to the pavilion was as effective as any that he had essayed in his more villainous roles.

I managed another streaky four before being bowled, and when I returned to the 'pavilion' (the gardener's shed), Tom sportingly said, 'You should stick to writing, Ruskin'—quite forgetting that I had out-scored him!

After that, I had to pay for the refreshments and contribute towards the prize money (won by the Dhobi Ghat Team), and all this necessitated another trip to the bank before closing time.

★

I was home well in time for lunch. My favourite rajma-bean curry, with hot chapattis and mango pickle. As it was a Saturday, the kids were home from school, and we all tucked in—except for Gautam who was on a hunger-strike because his promised Saturday ice cream was missing. Then his father arrived and took us for a drive to Dhanaulti, where there was ice cream aplenty.

Gone are the days when a picnic involved preparing and packing a lunch basket, and then trudging off into the wilderness on a hot and dusty road. People don't walk anymore. They get into their cars and drive out to a crowded 'picnic spot' where dhabas will provide you with national dishes such as chowmein or pizzas. While Indian cuisine has taken over Britain, Chinese and Italian dishes have conquered Indian palates. There's globalisation for you.

But I miss those picnics of old. They were leisurely, strung-out affairs. We seemed to have more time on our hands and a picnic meant an entire day's outing.

In Simla we picnicked at the Brockhurst tennis courts (now apartment buildings), or out at Jutogh or Summer Hill, or beyond Chota Simla; but not at Jakko, where the monkeys—hundreds of them—were inclined to join in.

In Dehradun we picnicked at Sulphur Springs, or in the hills near Rajpura, or on the banks of the Tons or Suswa rivers. You could also go fishing at Raiwala, just before the Song joins the Ganga. Equipped with rod and line, some friends and I went fishing there, but being inexpert, caught nothing. Some soldiers who were camping there had caught dozens of fish (by stunning them with explosives, I'm afraid) and were generous enough to give us a couple of large singharas. We returned to Dehra with our 'catch', and impressed friends and neighbours with our prowess as anglers.

Here in Mussoorie there was Mossy Falls, and other more distant falls: the Company Bagh, Clouds End, Haunted Houses and the banks of the little Aglar river.

I won't go down to the Aglar again, at least not on foot. Climbing up, ascending from 2,000 to 7,000 feet within a distance of three or four miles takes it out of you. On my first visit, some thirty years ago, I was accompanied by several school children. On our way back, we took the wrong path and lost our way (a frequent occurrence when I'm put in charge), and it was past ten o'clock when we were located by a bunch of anxious and angry parents accompanied by villagers who'd seen me going down. Fortunately, there was a full moon and there were no mishaps on the steep and stony path.

We went to bed hungry that night.

On another occasion, well provisioned with parathas, various sabzi, pickles, boiled eggs and bananas, two young friends—Kuku and Deepak—and I, tramped down to the Aglar and spread ourselves out on a grassy knoll. A pool of limpid water looked cool and inviting. We removed our clothes and plunged into the water. Great fun! We romped about, quite oblivious to what might be happening to our provisions. Then one of us looked up and yelled, 'Monkeys!' At least six of them were tucking into our lunch. We scrambled up the bank, and the monkeys fled, taking with them the remains of the parathas, the last bananas, and most of our underwear. They had left the pickle for us.

We were a sorry looking threesome by the time we returned to the town. But we did not go to bed hungry. We had enough money between us for a meal at Neelam's—then the most popular restaurant on the Mall—and we did full justice to various kababs, koftas, tikkas and tandoori rotis.

By now my readers will have come to the conclusion that I am perpetually persecuted by monkeys. And you would not be far wrong, gentle reader. Even as I write, I see one grinning at me from my window. Fortunately the window is closed and he cannot get in. I stick my tongue out at him, and he takes off, finding me far more hideous than his friends and relations.

But it wasn't always like that. Some years ago, when I lived in Maplewood, on the edge of the forest, a little girl monkey would sometimes perch shyly on the windowsill and study me with friendly curiosity. The rest of her tribe showed no interest in me as a person, but this little girl—and I think of her as a human rather than as a monkey—would turn up every morning while I was at my typewriter, and sit there quietly, her eyes intent on me as I tapped out a story or article. Perhaps it was the typewriter that fascinated her. I like to think it was my blue eyes. She had blue eyes too!

Now it isn't often that girls take a fancy to me, but I like to think that the little monkey had a crush on me. Her eyes had a gentle, appealing look, and she would make little chuckling sounds that I took for intimate conversation. If I approached, she would leap onto the walnut tree just outside the window and gesture to me to join her there. But my tree-climbing days were already over; and besides, I was afraid of her peers and parents.

One day I came into the room and found her at the typewriter, playing with the keys. When she saw me, she returned to the window and looked guilty. I looked down at the sheet in my machine. Had she been trying to give me a message? It read something like this—*!;!_l;:0—and there it broke off. I'm convinced she was trying to write the word 'love'.

However, I never did find out for sure, and the tribe went away, taking my girl friend with her. I never saw her again. Perhaps they married her off.

Talking of marriages, I am often asked by sympathetic readers why I never married. Now that's a long, sad story which would be out of place here, but I can tell you the story of my Uncle Bertie and why he never married.

As a young man, Uncle Bertie worked at the Ishapore rifle factory, which is just outside Kolkata. In pre-Independence days, Ishapore had a large Anglo-Indian and European community, many of whom were employed in the factory. Uncle Bertie was an impetuous fellow. He had a bit of a fling with a girl who lived across the road, and after a romp in the nearest mango-grove, he asked her to marry him. She agreed with alacrity. She was older than him, much taller, and her figure—46, 46, 46—would have been the envy of Marlene Dietrich or Marilyn Monroe. The girl's parents were agreeable, and everything had been arranged when Bertie Bond began to have second thoughts. He was always one for second thoughts. His brief infatuation over, he began to wonder what he had seen in the girl in the first place. She liked going to dances and Bertie couldn't dance. Her reading was limited to film magazines such as *Hollywood Romance*, while Bertie read Maxim Gorky and Emile Zola. She could not cook. Nor could Bertie. And khansamas were expensive. She liked to go shopping and Bertie's salary was three hundred rupees per month.

The banns were announced, the great day came around, and the church filled up with friends, relatives and well-wishers. The padre put on his gown and prepared to take the wedding service. The bride was present, arrayed in the white wedding dress in which her mother had been married. But there was no sign of Bertie. Half an hour, an hour, two hours passed. The bridegroom could not be found.

He had, in fact, fled to Calcutta, and had gone underground. He remained underground for sometime, emerging from hiding only in order to take a job at the docks in Ishapore. Everyone was waiting for him to return. They had varied and interesting ideas of what they would do to him. Some of them are still waiting.

'Marriage,' said Oscar Wilde, 'is a romance in which the hero dies in the first chapter.'

Uncle Bertie made his exit in the Preface.

6

IF MICE COULD ROW

If mice could roar
And elephants soar
And trees grow up in the sky,
If tigers would dine
On biscuits and wine,
And the fattest of folk could fly!

If pebbles could sing
And bells never ring
And teachers were lost in the post;
If a tortoise could run
And losses be won
And bullies be buttered on toast;

If a song brought a shower
And a gun grew a flower,
Our world would be better than most.

7

IN SEARCH OF SWEET-PEAS

If someone were to ask me to choose between writing an essay on the Taj Mahal or on the last rose of the summer, I'd take the rose—even if it was down to its last petal. Beautiful, cold, white marble leaves me—well, just a little cold....Roses are warm and fragrant, and almost every flower I know, wild or cultivated, has its own unique quality, whether it be subtle fragrance or arresting colour or liveliness of design. Unfortunately, winter has come to the Himalayas, and the hillsides are now brown and dry, the only colour being that of the red sorrel growing from the limestone rocks. Even my small garden looks rather forlorn, with the year's last dark-eyed nesturtium looking every bit like the Lone Ranger surveying the surrounding wilderness from his saddle. The marigolds have dried in the sun and tomorrow I will gather the seeds. The beanstalk that grew rampant during the monsoon is now down to a few yellow leaves and empty bean-pods.

'This won't do,' I told myself the other day. 'I must have flowers.' Prem, who had been to the valley town of Dehra the previous week, had made me even more restless, because he had spoken of masses of sweet-peas in full bloom in the garden of one of the town's public schools. Down in the plains, winter is the best time for gardens, and I remembered my grandmother's house in Dehra, with its long rows of hollyhocks, neatly-stalked sweet-peas and beds ablaze with red salvia and antirrhunum. Neither grandmother nor the house are there anymore. But surely there are other beautiful gardens, I mused, and maybe I could visit the school where Prem had seen the sweet-peas. It was a long time since I had enjoyed their delicate fragrance.

So I took the bus down the hill, and throughout the two-hour journey, I dozed and dreamt of gardens—cottage gardens in the English countryside, tropical gardens in Florida, Mughal gardens in Kashmir, the Hanging Gardens of Babylon—what had they been like, I wondered.

And then we were in Dehra, and I got down from the bus and walked down the dusty, busy road to the school Prem had told me about.

It was encircled by a high wall, and, tip-toeing, I could see playing fields and extensive school buildings and, in the far distance, a dollop of colour which may have been a garden. Prem's eyesight was obviously better than mine.

Anyway, I made my way to a wrought iron gate that would have done justice to a medieval fortress, and found it chained and locked. On the other side stood a tough looking guard, with a rifle.

'May I enter?' I asked.

'Sorry, sir, today is holiday. No school today.'

'I don't want to attend classes, I want to see the sweet-peas.'

'Kitchen is on the other side of the ground.'

'Not green peas. Sweet-peas. I'm looking for the garden.'

'I am guard here.'

'Garden.'

'No garden, only guard.'

I tried telling him that I was an old boy of the school and that I was visiting the town after a long interval. This was true up to a point, because I had once been admitted to this very school, and after one day's attendance had insisted on going back to my old school. The guard was unimpressed. And perhaps it was poetic justice that the gates were barred to me now.

Disconsolate, I strolled down the main road, past a garage, a cinema, a row of cheap eating houses and tea shops. Behind the shops there seemed to be a park of sorts, but you couldn't see much of it from the road because of the buildings, the press of the people, and the passing trucks and buses. But I found the entrance, unbarred this time, and struggled through patches of overgrown shrubbery until, like Alice after finding the golden key to the little door in the wall, I looked upon a lovely little garden.

There were no sweet-peas, true, and the small fountain was dry. But around it, filling a large circular bed, were masses of bright yellow Californian poppies!

They stood out like sunshine after the rain, and my heart leapt as Wordsworth's must have done when he saw his daffodils. I found myself oblivious to the sounds of the bazaar and the road, just as the people outside seemed oblivious to this little garden. It was as though it had been waiting here all the time. Waiting for me to come by and discover it.

I am very fortunate. Something like this is always happening to me. As grandmother often said, 'When one door closes, another door opens.' And while one gate had been closed upon the sweet-peas, another had opened on Californian poppies.

Trees make you feel younger. And the older the tree, the younger you feel.

Whenever I pass beneath the old tamarind tree standing sentinel in the middle of Dehra's busiest street crossing, the years fall away and I am a boy again, sitting on the railing that circled the tree, while across the road, Granny ascended the steps of the Allahabad Bank, where she kept her savings.

The bank is still there, but the surroundings have changed, the traffic and the noise is far greater than it used to be, and I wouldn't dream of sauntering across the road as casually as I would have done in those days. The press of people is greater too, reflecting the tenfold increase in population that has taken place in this and other north Indian towns during the last forty years. But the old tamarind has managed to survive it all. As long as it stands, as long as its roots still cling to Dehra's rich soil, I shall feel confident that my own roots are well embedded in this old valley town.

There was a time when almost every Indian village had its spreading banyan tree, in whose generous shade, schoolteachers conducted open-air classes, village elders met to discuss matters of moment, and itinerant merchants spread out their ware. Squirrels, birds of many kinds, flying-foxes, and giant beetles, are just some of the many inhabitants of this gentle giant. Ancient banyan trees are still to be found in some parts of the country; but as villages grow into towns, and towns into cities, the banyan is gradually disappearing. It needs a lot of space for its aerial roots to travel and support it, and space is now at a premium.

If you can't find a banyan, a mango grove is a wonderful place for a quiet stroll or an afternoon siesta. In traditional paintings, it is often the haunt of young lovers. But if the mangoes are ripening, there is not much privacy in a mango grove. Parrots, crows, monkeys and small boys are all attempting to evade the watchman who uses an empty gasoline tin as a drum to frighten away these intruders.

The mango and the banyan don't grow above the foothills, and here in the mountains, the more familiar trees are the Himalayan oaks, horse-chestnuts, rhododendrons, pines and deodars. The deodar (from the Sanskrit dev-dar, meaning Tree of God) resembles the cedar of Lebanon, and can grow to a great height in a few hundred years. There are a number of giant deodars on the outskirts of Mussoorie, where I live, and they make the town seem quite young. Mussoorie is only 160 years old. The deodars are at least twice that age.

These are gregarious trees—they like being among their own kind—and a forest of deodars is an imposing sight. When a mountain is covered with them, they look like an army on the march: the only kind of army one would like to see marching over the mountains! Although the world has already lost over half its forest cover, these sturdy giants look as though they are going to be around a long time, given half a chance.

The world's oldest trees, a species of pine, grow in California and have been known to live up to five thousand years. Is that why Californians look so young?

The oldest tree I have seen is an ancient mulberry growing at Joshimath, a small temple town in the Himalayas. It is known as the Kalp-Vriksha or Immortal Tree. The Hindu sage, Sankaracharya, is said to have meditated beneath it in the sixteenth century. These ancient sages always found a suitable tree beneath which they could meditate. The Buddha favoured a banyan tree, while Hindu ascetics are still to be found sitting cross-legged beneath peepal trees. Peepals are just right in summer, because the slender heart-shaped leaves catch the slightest breeze and send cool currents down to the thinker below.

Personally, I prefer contemplation to meditation. I am happy to stand back from the great mulberry and study its awesome proportions. Not a tall tree, but it has an immense girth—my three-room apartment in Mussoorie would have fitted quite snugly into it. A small temple beside the tree looked very tiny indeed, and the children playing among its protruding roots could have been kittens.

As I said, I'm not one for meditating beneath trees, but that's really because something always happens to me when I try. I don't know how the great sages managed, but I find it difficult to concentrate when a Rhesus monkey comes up to me and stares me in the face. Or when a horse-chestnut bounces off my head. Or when a cloud of pollen slides off the branch of a deodar and down the back of my shirt. Or when a woodpecker starts hammering away a few feet up the trunk from where I sit. I expect the great ones were immune to all this arboreal activity. I'm just a nature-lover, easily distracted by the caterpillar crawling up my leg.

And so I am happy to stand back and admire the 'good, green-hatted people', as a visitor from another planet described the trees in a story by R.L. Stevenson. Especially the old trees. They have seen a lot of odd humans coming and going, and they know I'm just a seventy-year-old boy without any pretensions to being a sage.

8

THE REGIMENTAL MYNA*

In my grandfather's time, British soldiers stationed in India were very fond of keeping pets, and there were few barrack-rooms where pets were not to be found. Dogs and cats were the most common, but birds were also great favourites.

In one instance, a bird was not only the pet of a barrack-room but of a whole regiment. His owner was my grandfather, Private Bond, a soldier of the line who had come out to India with the King's Own Scottish Rifles.

The bird was a myna, common enough in India, and Grandfather named it Dickens after his favourite author. Dickens came into Grandfather's possession when quite young,

---

* The grandfather referred to here is my soldier grandfather and not my Dehradun grandfather.

and he was soon a favourite with all the men in the barracks at Meerut, where the regiment was stationed. Meerut was hot and dusty; the curries were hot and spicy; the General in command was hot-tempered and crusty. Keeping a pet was almost the sole recreation for the men in barracks.

Because he was tamed so young, Dickens (or Dicky for short) never learned to pick up food for himself. Instead, just like a baby bird, he took his meals from Grandfather's mouth. And other men used to feed him in the same way. When Dickens was hungry, he asked for food by sitting on Grandfather's shoulders, flapping his wings rapidly, and opening his beak.

Dicky was never caged, and as soon as he was able to fly he attended all parades, watched the rations being issued, and was present on every occasion which brought the soldiers out of their barracks. When out in the country, he would follow the regiment or party, flying from shoulder to shoulder, or from tree to tree, always keeping a sharp look-out for his enemies, the hawks.

Sometimes he would choose a mounted officer as a companion; but after the manoeuvres were over he would return to Grandfather's shoulder.

One day there was to be a General's inspection, and the Colonel gave orders that Dicky was to be confined, so that he wouldn't appear on parade.

'Lock him away somewhere, Bond,' the Colonel snapped. 'We can't have him flapping all over the parade-ground.'

Dickens was put into a storeroom, with the windows closed and the door locked. But while the General's inspection was going on, the mess orderly, who wanted something from the storeroom and knew where to find the key, opened the door.

Out flew Dickens. He made straight for the parade-ground, greatly excited at being let out and chattering loudly.

Dicky must have thought the General had something to do with his detention, or else he may have felt an explanation was due to him. Whatever his reasoning, he chose to alight on the General's pith helmet, between the plumes.

Here he chattered faster than ever, much to the surprise of the General, who was obliged to take his helmet off before he could dislodge the bird.

'What the dickens!' exclaimed the General, going purple in the face—for Dicky had discharged his breakfast between the plumes of the helmet.

Meanwhile, Dicky had flown to the Colonel's shoulder to make further complaints, to the great delight of the men.

'Fall out, Bond!' the Colonel screamed. 'Take this bird away—for good! I don't want to see it again!'

A crestfallen Private Bond returned to the barracks with Dicky, wondering what to do next. To part with Dicky, or even to cage him, was out of the question.

But Grandfather was not the only one who loved Dickens. He was also highly popular with the entire battalion. In the end, Grandfather decided to ask his Captain to bring him before the Colonel so he could ask forgiveness for Dicky's behaviour.

The Colonel gave Private Bond and his Captain a patient hearing. Then the Colonel consulted his officers and decided that the bird could stay—provided he was taken on as a serving member of the regiment!

Dickens' popularity was not surprising, as he was highly intelligent. He knew the men of his own regiment from those of others, and would only associate with the Scottish Rifles. Even in the drill season, when there were as many as twenty regiments in camp, Dicky never made a mistake.

Dickens had a unique method of getting from one part of the camp to another. Instead of flying over the top of the camp, he would go in stages from tent to tent, flying very low, sheltering in each one, then peeping out and looking carefully for hawks before moving on to the next.

One day Grandfather was admitted to hospital with malaria. Dicky couldn't find him anywhere, and searched and searched all over the camp in great distress. The hospital was a couple of kilometres away from the barracks, and it wasn't until the third day of searching that Dickens finally discovered Grandfather lying there.

From then on, for as long as Grandfather was on the sick list, Dicky spent his time at the hospital. An upturned helmet was placed on a shelf for him near Grandfather's bed, and Dickens spent the night inside it. As soon as Grandfather was discharged from the hospital, Dickens left as well, and never returned, not even for a visit.

In 1888, the regiment got orders to proceed to Calcutta, en route for Burma, where it was to take part in the Chin Lushai Expedition. All pets had to be left behind, and Dickens was no exception.

But Dicky had his own views on the subject.

The regiment travelled in stages, marching along the Grand Trunk Road, moving at night and going into rest camps for the day.

Dickens caught up on the third day. He arrived in camp after a journey of more than three hundred kilometres—dull, dejected and starving, as he still depended on being fed from Grandfather's mouth.

Route-marching and travelling by train (the railway was just beginning to spread across India), the battalion finally reached Calcutta. From there, contrary to orders, Dickens embarked for Burma along with the soldiers.

On board the ship, Dickens would amuse himself by peeping from the portholes, and flapping from one to the other. He would also go up on deck, and sometimes even took experimental flights out to sea. But one day he was caught in a gale and had such difficulty getting back to the ship that he gave up that kind of adventuring.

Dickens stayed with his regiment all through the expedition and the campaign. Many of his soldier friends lost their lives, but Grandfather and Dickens survived the fighting and returned safely to Calcutta.

Grandfather, now a Corporal, was given six months' home leave, along with the rest of the regiment. This meant sailing home to England.

During the first part of the voyage, Dicky was his usual cheerful self. But when the ship left the Suez Canal, the weather grew cold, and he was no longer to be seen on the yardarms or on the bridge with the captain. He even lost interest in going on deck with Grandfather, preferring to stay with the parrots on the waste deck.

After the ship passed Gibraltar, Dickens went below. He never came on deck again.

Dickens was laid out in a Huntley and Palmer's biscuit tin, and buried at sea. Not, perhaps, with full military honours, but certainly to the sound of Grandfather's bagpipes, playing *The Last Post*.

5

MONKEY TROUBLE

Grandfather bought Tutu from a street entertainer for the sum of ten rupees. The man had three monkeys. Tutu was the smallest, but the most mischievous. She was tied up most of the time. The little monkey looked so miserable with a collar and chain that Grandfather decided it would be much happier in our home. Grandfather had a weakness for keeping unusual pets. It was a habit that I, at the age of eight or nine, used to encourage.

Grandmother at first objected to having a monkey in the house. 'You have enough pets as it is,' she said, referring to Grandfather's goat, several white mice, and a small tortoise.

'But I don't have any,' I said.

'You're wicked enough for two monkeys. One boy in the house is all I can take.'

'Ah, but Tutu isn't a boy,' said Grandfather triumphantly. 'This is a little girl monkey!'

Grandmother gave in. She had always wanted a little girl in the house. She believed girls were less troublesome than boys. Tutu was to prove her wrong.

She was a pretty little monkey. Her bright eyes sparkled with mischief beneath deep-set eyebrows. And her teeth, which were a pearly white, were often revealed in a grin that frightened the wits out of Aunt Ruby, whose nerves had already suffered from the presence of Grandfather's pet python in the house at Lucknow. But this was Dehra, my grandparents' house, and aunts and uncles had to put up with our pets.

Tutu's hands had a dried-up look, as though they had been pickled in the sun for many years. One of the first things I taught her was to shake hands, and this she insisted on doing with all who visited the house. Peppery Major Malik would have to stoop and shake hands with Tutu before he could enter the drawing room, otherwise Tutu would climb onto his shoulder and stay there, roughing up his hair and playing with his moustache.

Uncle Ken couldn't stand any of our pets and took a particular dislike to Tutu, who was always making faces at him. But as Uncle Ken was never in a job for long, and depended on Grandfather's good-natured generosity, he had to shake hands with Tutu, like everyone else.

Tutu's fingers were quick and wicked. And her tail, while adding to her good looks (Grandfather believed a tail would add to anyone's good looks!), also served as a third hand. She could use it to hang from a branch, and it was capable of scooping up any delicacy that might be out of reach of her hands.

Aunt Ruby had not been informed of Tutu's arrival. Loud shrieks from her bedroom brought us running to see what was wrong. It was only Tutu trying on Aunt Ruby's petticoats! They were much too large, of course, and when Aunt Ruby entered the room, all she saw was a faceless white blob jumping up and down on the bed.

We disentangled Tutu and soothed Aunt Ruby. I gave Tutu a bunch of sweet-peas to make her happy. Granny didn't like anyone plucking her sweet-peas, so I took some from Major Malik's garden while he was having his afternoon siesta.

Then Uncle Ken complained that his hairbrush was missing. We found Tutu sunning herself on the back verandah, using the hairbrush to scratch her armpits.

I took it from her and handed it back to Uncle Ken with an apology; but he flung the brush away with an oath.

'Such a fuss about nothing,' I said. 'Tutu doesn't have fleas!'

'No, and she bathes more often than Ken,' said Grandfather, who had borrowed Aunt Ruby's shampoo to give Tutu a bath.

All the same, Grandmother objected to Tutu being given the run of the house. Tutu had to spend her nights in the out-house, in the company of the goat. They got on quite well, and it was not long before Tutu was seen sitting comfortably on the back of the goat, while the goat roamed the back garden in search of its favourite grass.

The day Grandfather had to visit Meerut to collect his railway pension, he decided to take Tutu and me along to keep us both out of mischief, he said. To prevent Tutu from wandering about on the train, causing inconvenience to passengers, she was provided with a large black travelling bag. This, with some straw at the bottom, became her compartment. Grandfather and I paid for our seats, and we took Tutu along as hand baggage.

There was enough space for Tutu to look out of the bag occasionally, and to be fed with bananas and biscuits, but she could not get her hands through the opening and the canvas was too strong for her to bite her way through.

Tutu's efforts to get out only had the effect of making the bag roll about on the floor or occasionally jump into the air—an exhibition that attracted a curious crowd of onlookers at the Dehra and Meerut railway stations.

Anyway, Tutu remained in the bag as far as Meerut, but while Grandfather was producing our tickets at the turnstile, she suddenly poked her head out of the bag and gave the ticket collector a wide grin.

The poor man was taken aback. But, with great presence of mind and much to Grandfather's annoyance, he said, 'Sir, you have a dog with you. You'll have to buy a ticket for it.'

'It's not a dog!' said Grandfather indignantly. 'This is a baby monkey of the species *macacus-mischievous*, closely related to the human species *homus-horriblis*! And there is no charge for babies!'

'It's as big as a cat,' said the ticket collector. 'Cats and dogs have to be paid for.'

'But, I tell you, it's only a baby!' protested Grandfather.

'Have you a birth certificate to prove that?' demanded the ticket collector.

'Next, you'll be asking to see her mother,' snapped Grandfather.

In vain did he take Tutu out of the bag. In vain did he try to prove that a young monkey did not qualify as a dog or a cat or even as a quadruped. Tutu was classified as a dog by the ticket collector, and five rupees were handed over as her fare.

Then Grandfather, just to get his own back, took from his pocket the small tortoise that he sometimes carried about, and said: 'And what must I pay for this, since you charge for all creatures great and small?'

The ticket collector looked closely at the tortoise, prodded it with his forefinger, gave Grandfather a triumphant look, and said, 'No charge, sir. It is not a dog!'

Winters in north India can be very cold. A great treat for Tutu on winter evenings was the large bowl of hot water given to her by Grandfather for a bath. Tutu would cunningly test the temperature with her hand, then gradually step into the bath, first one foot, then the other (as she had seen me doing) until she was in the water upto her neck.

Once comfortable, she would take the soap in her hands or feet and rub herself all over. When the water became cold, she would get out and run as quickly as she could to the kitchen fire in order to dry herself. If anyone laughed at her during this performance, Tutu's feelings would be hurt and she would refuse to go on with the bath.

One day Tutu almost succeeded in boiling herself alive. Grandmother had left a large kettle on the fire for tea. And Tutu, all by herself and with nothing better to do, decided to remove the lid. Finding the water just warm enough for a bath, she got in, with her head sticking out from the open kettle.

This was fine for a while, until the water began to get heated. Tutu raised herself a little. But finding it cold outside, she sat down again. She continued hopping up and down for some time, until Grandmother returned and hauled her, half-boiled, out of the kettle.

'What's for tea today?' asked Uncle Ken gleefully. 'Boiled eggs and a half-boiled monkey?'

But Tutu was none the worse for the adventure and continued to bathe more regularly than Uncle Ken.

Aunt Ruby was a frequent taker of baths. This met with Tutu's approval—so much so that, one day, when Aunt Ruby had finished shampooing her hair, she looked up through a lather of bubbles and soap-suds to see Tutu sitting opposite her in the bath, following her example.

One day Aunt Ruby took us all by surprise. She announced that she had become engaged. We had always thought Aunt Ruby would never marry—she had often said so herself—but it appeared that the right man had now come along in the person of Rocky Fernandes, a schoolteacher from Goa.

Rocky was a tall, firm-jawed, good-natured man, a couple of years younger than Aunt Ruby. He had a fine baritone voice and sang in the manner of the great Nelson Eddy. As

Grandmother liked baritone singers, Rocky was soon in her good books.

'But what on earth does he see in her?' Uncle Ken wanted to know.

'More than any girl has seen in you!' snapped Grandmother. 'Ruby's a fine girl. And they're both teachers. Maybe they can start a school of their own.'

Rocky visited the house quite often and brought me chocolates and cashewnuts, of which he seemed to have an unlimited supply. He also taught me several marching songs. Naturally, I approved of Rocky. Aunt Ruby won my grudging admiration for having made such a wise choice.

One day I overheard them talking of going to the bazaar to buy an engagement ring. I decided I would go along, too. But as Aunt Ruby had made it clear that she did not want me around, I decided that I had better follow at a discreet distance. Tutu, becoming aware that a mission of some importance was under way, decided to follow me. But as I had not invited her along, she too decided to keep out of sight.

Once in the crowded bazaar, I was able to get quite close to Aunt Ruby and Rocky without being spotted. I waited until they had settled down in a large jewellery shop before sauntering past and spotting them, as though by accident. Aunt Ruby wasn't too pleased at seeing me, but Rocky waved and called out, 'Come and join us! Help your aunt choose a beautiful ring!'

The whole thing seemed to be a waste of good money, but I did not say so—Aunt Ruby was giving me one of her more unloving looks.

'Look, these are pretty!' I said, pointing to some cheap, bright agates set in white metal. But Aunt Ruby wasn't looking. She was immersed in a case of diamonds.

'Why not a ruby for Aunt Ruby?' I suggested, trying to please her.

'That's her lucky stone,' said Rocky. 'Diamonds are the thing for engagements.' And he started singing a song about a diamond being a girl's best friend.

While the jeweller and Aunt Ruby were sifting through the diamond rings, and Rocky was trying out another tune, Tutu had slipped into the shop without being noticed by anyone but me. A little squeal of delight was the first sign she gave of her presence. Everyone looked up to see her trying on a pretty necklace.

'And what are those stones?' I asked.

'They look like pearls,' said Rocky.

'They are pearls,' said the shopkeeper, making a grab for them.

'It's that dreadful monkey!' cried Aunt Ruby. 'I knew that boy would bring him here!'

The necklace was already adorning Tutu's neck. I thought she looked rather nice in them, but she gave us no time to admire the effect. Springing out of our reach, Tutu dodged around Rocky, slipped between my legs, and made for the crowded road. I ran after her, shouting to her to stop, but she wasn't listening.

There were no branches to assist Tutu in her progress, but she used the heads and shoulders of people as springboards and so made rapid headway through the bazaar.

The jeweller left his shop and ran after us. So did Rocky. So did several bystanders, who had seen the incident. And others, who had no idea what it was all about, joined in the chase. As Grandfather used to say, 'In a crowd, everyone plays follow-the-leader, even when they don't know who's leading.' Not everyone knew that the leader was Tutu. Only the front runners could see her.

She tried to make her escape speedier by leaping onto the back of a passing scooterist. The scooter swerved into a fruit stall and came to a standstill under a heap of bananas, while the scooterist found himself in the arms of an indignant fruitseller. Tutu peeled a banana and ate part of it, before deciding to move on.

From an awning she made an emergency landing on a washerman's donkey. The donkey promptly panicked and rushed down the road, while bundles of washing fell by the wayside. The washerman joined in the chase. Children on their way to school decided that here was something better to do than attend classes. With shouts of glee, they soon overtook their panting elders.

Tutu finally left the bazaar and took a road leading in the direction of our house. But knowing that she would be caught and locked up once she got home, she decided to end the chase by ridding herself of the necklace. Deftly removing it from her neck, she flung it in the small canal that ran down the road.

The jeweller, with a cry of anguish, plunged into the canal. So did Rocky. So did I. So did several other people, both adults and children. It was to be a treasure hunt!

Some twenty minutes later, Rocky shouted, 'I've found it!' Covered in mud, water-lilies, ferns and tadpoles, we emerged from the canal, and Rocky presented the necklace to the relieved shopkeeper.

Everyone trudged back to the bazaar to find Aunt Ruby waiting in the shop, still trying to make up her mind about a suitable engagement ring.

Finally the ring was bought, the engagement was announced, and a date was set for the wedding.

'I don't want that monkey anywhere near us on our wedding day,' declared Aunt Ruby.

'We'll lock her up in the out-house,' promised Grandfather. 'And we'll let her out only after you've left for your honeymoon.'

A few days before the wedding I found Tutu in the kitchen, helping Grandmother prepare the wedding cake. Tutu often helped with the cooking and, when Grandmother wasn't looking, added herbs, spices, and other interesting items to the pots—so that occasionally we found a chilli in the custard or an onion in the jelly or a strawberry floating in the chicken soup.

Sometimes these additions improved a dish, sometimes they did not. Uncle Ken lost a tooth when he bit firmly into a sandwich which contained walnut shells.

I'm not sure exactly what went into that wedding cake when Grandmother wasn't looking—she insisted that Tutu was always very well-behaved in the kitchen—but I did spot Tutu stirring in some red chilli sauce, bitter gourd seeds, and a generous helping of egg-shells!

It's true that some of the guests were not seen for several days after the wedding, but no one said anything against the cake. Most people thought it had an interesting flavour.

The great day dawned, and the wedding guests made their way to the little church that stood on the outskirts of Dehra— a town with a church, two mosques, and several temples.

I had offered to dress Tutu up as a bridesmaid and bring her along, but no one except Grandfather thought it was a good idea. So I was an obedient boy and locked Tutu in the out-house. I did, however, leave the skylight open a little. Grandmother had always said that fresh air was good for growing children, and I thought Tutu should have her share of it.

The wedding ceremony went without a hitch. Aunt Ruby looked a picture, and Rocky looked like a film star.

Grandfather played the organ, and did so with such gusto that the small choir could hardly be heard. Grandmother cried a little, I sat quietly in a corner, with the little tortoise on my lap.

When the service was over, we trooped out into the sunshine and made our way back to the house for the reception.

The feast had been laid out on tables in the garden. As the gardener had been left in charge, everything was in order. Tutu was on her best behaviour. She had, it appeared, used the skylight to avail of more fresh air outside, and now sat beside the three-tier wedding cake, guarding it against crows, squirrels and the goat. She greeted the guests with squeals of delight.

It was too much for Aunt Ruby. She flew at Tutu in a rage. And Tutu, sensing that she was not welcome, leapt away, taking with her the top tier of the wedding cake.

Led by Major Malik, we followed her into the orchard, only to find that she had climbed to the top of the jackfruit tree. From there she proceeded to pelt us with bits of wedding cake. She had also managed to get hold of a bag of confetti, and when she ran out of cake she showered us with confetti.

'That's more like it!' said the good-humoured Rocky. 'Now let's return to the party, folks!'

Uncle Ken remained with Major Malik, determined to chase Tutu away. He kept throwing stones into the tree, until he received a large piece of cake bang on his nose. Muttering threats, he returned to the party, leaving the Major to do battle.

When the festivities were finally over, Uncle Ken took the old car out of the garage and drove up the veranda steps. He was going to drive Aunt Ruby and Rocky to the nearby hill resort of Mussoorie, where they would have their honeymoon.

Watched by family and friends, Aunt Ruby climbed into the back seat. She waved regally to everyone. She leant out of the window and offered me her cheek and I had to kiss her farewell. Everyone wished them luck.

As Rocky burst into song, Uncle Ken opened the throttle and stepped on the accelerator. The car shot forward in a cloud of dust.

Rocky and Aunt Ruby continued to wave to us. And so did Tutu, from her perch on the rear bumper! She was clutching a bag in her hands and showering confetti on all who stood in the driveway.

'They don't know Tutu's with them!' I exclaimed.

'She'll go all the way to Mussoorie! Will Aunt Ruby let her stay with them?'

'Tutu might ruin the honeymoon,' said Grandfather. 'But don't worry—our Ken will bring her back!'

9

FROGS IN THE FOUNTAIN

Marigolds grew almost everywhere in our beautiful country, and they are constantly in demand—at festivals, marriages, religious ceremonies, arrivals and departures, functions of all kinds. If you happen to be a guest of honour on a public occasion, be prepared to be smothered in garlands of marigolds. I am a little wary of these welcoming garlands because on one occasion a slumbering bee, nestling between the petals, flew out and stung me under my chin. It made for a very short speech.

When I told young Gautam about this incident, he asked, 'Is that how you got your double chin?'

Actually the double chin came from my grandmother, who was a large, generously proportioned lady with a number of chins. Gautam and his sister Shrishti like to play with my double chin, but I would never have dared touch my old Granny on her chin or anywhere else. She was a stern, reserved woman, with a strict Victorian upbringing, who believed that little boys should speak only when spoken to.

She fed us reasonably well—she kept a great khansama—but she did not believe in second helpings, with the result that I spent the rest of my life indulging in second helpings.

Two mutton koftas were all that I was allowed with my plate of rice. I liked koftas—still do—and it was painful for a small boy to have to stop at two. Now that I am a grown man with an independent source of income, I help myself to four! Who can stop me?

Dr Bhist, who drops in to see me once a year, remarked that I looked overweight and that I should cut down on my food intake.

'What did you have for lunch?' he asked.

'Kofta curry and rice.'

'How much rice?'

'Just two small helpings.'

'And how many koftas?'

'Only four.'

'Don't have more than two,' he advised.

'Yes, Granny,' I said.

Dr Bhist gave me a puzzled look.

'Sorry,' I said, 'I thought you were my grandmother.'

Now he thinks I've got Alzheimer's.

★

FROGS IN THE FOUNTAIN

Talking of marigolds, Granny surrounded her house with them, as she believed they kept snakes away. Apparently snakes do not like their pungent aroma. I, too, believed in this folk lore until I was told (by an expert on reptiles) that snakes do not have a strong sense of smell and would be impervious to the scent of flowers or other odours. Maybe so, but I don't recall ever seeing a snake in Granny's garden, although I did see them elsewhere. However, we did have plenty of frogs, thanks to the disused fountain installed by my grandfather but neglected after his death.

The fountain hadn't functioned for a couple of years, but the little reservoir in which it stood had filled up with rain water and was now covered with water-lilies.

One day, after an expedition to the Canal Head Works, I brought home some small fish in a bucket and introduced them to the lily pond. I hadn't paid much attention to the tadpoles swimming around in the bucket.

Well, the fish died as they were used to fresh running water and not stagnant water; but the tadpoles did very well, and before long we had frogs leaping all over the place. Very soon the frogs multiplied. They would come into the veranda at night and keep us awake with their incessant singing and warbling.

'I can't sleep a wink,' complained Aunt Mabel, who was very sensitive to noise and allergic to choirs made up entirely of bass singers.

'They're serenading you,' I said. It was a long time since anyone had serenaded Aunt Mabel, a confirmed spinster in her early forties.

'They'll go away once the rains finish,' said Granny hopefully. But they did not go away. One day, screams came from the bathroom—Aunt Mabel screaming for help! Granny, the khansama and I ran to her aid, and discovered that the cause of her distress was a large frog swimming around in the potty.

I pulled the flush chain. There was a loud gurgling sound, a combination of frog and flush, and out jumped the frog straight into Aunt Mabel's arms. She left for Lucknow that day, saying she would be safer in a zoo, where her cousin was the superintendent.

Well, Granny hired some labourers to empty the lily pond and round up as many frogs as they could. They were put into baskets and taken to some mysterious destination.

'Perhaps they've been exported to China,' I mused, 'or even to France. They eat frogs there, don't they?'

'Only the legs,' said Granny.

But they hadn't been exported. The khansama told me later that the baskets had been opened and dumped near a pond behind the railway-station and before long they were all over the station waiting-rooms and platforms, until the stationmaster had a brilliant idea. He had the frogs rounded up by a number of street urchins who wanted to make a little pocket money; he then had them packed firmly into several well-ventilated boxes.

The crates were labelled 'To Lucknow Zoo—Attn: Superintendent sahib', and dispatched as a free gift.

'A zoo is the best place for creatures great and small,' opined our philosophical stationmaster, who had previously sent them a consignment of stray station dogs.

Strangely enough, Aunt Mabel would have preferred a crate of frogs to a bouquet of flowers. She was allergic to flowers. Apparently the pollen brought on sneezing fits.

A fear of flowers is called anthophobia, and Aunt Mabel suffered from it. She lived in constant terror of flowers. An innocent pansy made her think of the devil; a snapdragon reminded her of real dragons; the spear-like leaves of the iris were as real spears to her; and the golden-rod sent shivers down her spine. The ones that made her sneeze the most were hollyhock, cosmos, calendula, daisies of all kinds and chrysanthemums.

It was more than an allergy, it was an irrational but very real fear of flowers. Their very names terrified her. If I shouted 'thunder-lily!' she would turn pale and tremble like a leaf. If I whispered 'gladioli', she would let out a shriek. If I said 'dandelion!' she would get a rash. And if I exclaimed 'convolvulus!' she'd go into convulsions.

Small boys can be cruel, especially to aunts, and I was no exception. But teasing Aunt Mabel with flowers had a limited appeal for me. Instead, I used them for blackmail. If I needed money for the cinema, I would take Aunt Mabel a bunch of larkspur or candytuft. She would turn pale at my approach, push me out of her room, and hurriedly give me the price of a cinema ticket.

In Lucknow, she lived in a flat and was able to keep flowers at bay. But in Dehra she had to put up with Granny's garden, and Granny had no intention of doing away with her flower garden. After all, she was acknowledged to have the most luxuriant display of sweet-peas in town. Also Aunt Mabel stayed indoors most of the time, venturing out only in a tonga. She felt quite safe in Paltan Bazaar where there were no flowers apart from the cauliflowers on sale in the sabzi mandi, and even these she avoided.

So engraved was my aunt's phobia that she made everyone in the family promise that when she died there would be no flowers at her funeral. However, she did not really trust us to carry out her wishes, and this may have been the reason why she left India and chose to settle in Arizona, in an area where even the cacti had a hard time surviving. She'd found happiness at last.

I, on the other hand, cannot live without flowers. A little vase of bright yellow and orange nasturtiums rests on the corner of my desk, and every now and then I look up to refresh my eyes and mind by gazing at them. I have never been able to afford a large house with a garden (like Granny's, which was sold when she died) but I grow geraniums in my window and nasturtiums on the roof, and in the spring I throw cosmos seed on the hillside and some of them come up and reward me and others with autumn flowers.

Of course we all have our phobias, and some of the most interesting include bacteriophobia, a fear of germs;

mysophobia, a fear of dirt (I knew someone who would wash her hands thirty to forty times a day, even when she was at home and unoccupied); xenophobia, a fear of strangers; nyctophobia, a fear of darkness; agoraphobia, a fear of open spaces. The trouble is, most of us—men especially—hate to admit being afraid of anything. This fear of showing fear is a phobia in itself. The word for it is phobophobia.

My own particular phobia is a fear of lifts. As far as possible I will avoid entering a building where it is necessary to use a lift. If I do go in, I take the stairs. On one occasion I was incarcerated in a five-star hotel where there was no staircase. My room was on the seventeenth floor. I was forced to use the fire-escape! Now you know why I prefer to stay at the India International Centre whenever I'm in New Delhi: not because I have any intellectual pretensions, but because the building (god bless the architect) has only two floors.

Perhaps the best way of dealing with a phobia is to give in to it, admit it, tell everyone about your weakness, and enlist their support. I can tell people that I'm afraid of lifts. As most fellow humans are sympathetic by nature, they crowd into the lift to keep me company, and press all the right buttons—something I have never been able to do successfully in lifts, on cell phones or with ladies' corsets.

Company in a lift always makes me feel much better. I know I won't be alone when it crashes.

10

ON FOOT WITH FAITH

All my life I've been a walking person. To this day, I have neither owned nor driven a car, bus, tractor, aeroplane, motor-boat, scooter, truck, or steam-roller. Forced to make a choice, I would drive a steam-roller, because of its slow but solid progress and unhurried finality.

In my early teens, I did for a brief period ride a bicycle, until I rode into a bullock-cart and broke my arm; the accident only serving to underline my unsuitability for wheeled conveyance or any conveyance that is likely to take my feet off the ground. Although dreamy and absent-minded, I have never walked into a bullock-cart.

Perhaps there is something to be said for sun-signs. Mine being Taurus, I have, like the bull, always stayed close to grass, and have lived my life at my own leisurely pace, only being stirred into furious activity when goaded beyond endurance. I have every sympathy for bulls and none for bull-fighters.

I was born in the Kasauli Military Hospital in 1934, and was baptised in the little Anglican church which still stands in this hill-station. My father had done his schooling at the Lawrence Royal Military School, at Sanwar, a few miles away, but he had gone into 'tea' and then teaching, and at the time I was born, he was out of a job.

But my earliest memories are not of Kasauli, for we left when I was two or three months old; they are of Jamnagar, a small state in coastal Kathiawar, where my father took a job as English tutor to several young princes and princesses. This was in the tradition of Forster and Ackerley, but my father did not have literary ambitions, although after his death I was to come across a notebook filled with love poems addressed to my mother, presumably while they were courting.

This was where the walking really began, because Jamnagar was full of palaces and spacious lawns and gardens. And by the time I was three, I was exploring much of this territory on my own, with the result that I encountered my first cobra who, instead of striking me dead as the best fictional cobras are supposed to do, allowed me to pass.

Living as he did so close to the ground, and sensitive to every footfall, that intelligent snake must have known instinctively that I presented no threat, that I was just a small human discovering the use of his legs. Envious of the snake's swift gliding movements, I went indoors and tried crawling about on my belly, but I wasn't much good at it. Legs were better.

Amongst my father's pupils in one of these small states were three beautiful princesses. One of them was about my age, but the other two were older, and they were the ones at whose feet I worshipped. I think I was four or five when I had this crush on two 'older' girls—eight and ten respectively. At first I wasn't sure that they were girls, because they always wore jackets and trousers and kept their hair quite short. But my father told me they were girls, and he never lied to me.

My father's schoolroom and our own living quarters were located in one of the older palaces, situated in the midst of a veritable jungle of a garden. Here I could roam to my heart's content, amongst marigolds and cosmos growing rampant in the long grass. An ayah or a bearer was often sent post-haste after me, to tell me to beware of snakes and scorpions.

One of the books read to me as a child was a work called *Little Henry and His Bearer*, in which little Henry converts his servant to Christianity. I'm afraid something rather different happened to me. My ayah, bless her soul, taught me to eat paan and other forbidden delights from the bazaar, while the bearer taught me to abuse in choice Hindustani—an attribute that has stood me in good stead over the years.

Neither of my parents was overly religious, and religious tracts came my way far less frequently than they do today. (*Little Henry* was a gift from a distant aunt.) Today everyone seems to feel I have a soul worth saving, whereas when I was

a boy, I was left severely alone by both preachers and adults. In fact the only time I felt threatened by religion was a few years later when, visiting the aunt I have mentioned, I happened to fall down her steps and sprain my ankle. She gave me a triumphant look and said, 'See what happens when you don't go to church!'

My father was a good man. He taught me to read and write long before I started going to school, although it's true to say that I first learned to read upside down. This happened because I would sit on a stool in front of the three princesses, watching them read and write, and so the view I had of their books was an upside-down one; I still read that way occasionally, especially when a book begins to get boring.

My mother was at least twelve years younger than my father, and liked going out to parties and dances. She was quite happy to leave me in the care of the ayah and bearer and other servants. I had no objection to the arrangement. The servants indulged me, and so did my father, bringing me books, toys, comics, chocolates and of course stamps, when he returned from visits to Bombay.

Walking along the beach, collecting sea-shells, I got into the habit of staring hard at the ground, a habit which has stayed with me all my life. Apart from helping my thought processes, it also results in my picking up odd objects—coins, keys, broken bangles, marbles, pens, bits of crockery, pretty stones, ladybirds, feathers, snail-shells, sea-shells! Occasionally, of course, this habit results in my walking some way past my destination (if I happen to have one). And why not? It simply means discovering a new and different destination, sights and sounds that I might not have experienced had I concluded my walk exactly where it was supposed to end. And I am not looking at the ground all the time. Sensitive like the snake to approaching footfalls, I look up from time to time to examine the faces of passers-by just in case they have something they wish to say to me.

A bird singing in a bush or tree has my immediate attention; so does any unfamiliar flower or plant, particularly if it grows in an unusual place such as a crack in a wall or rooftop, or in a yard full of junk where I once found a rose-bush blooming on the roof of an old Ford car.

There are other kinds of walks that I shall come to later but it wasn't until I came to Dehra and my grandmother's house that I really found my feet as a walker.

In 1939, when World War II broke out, my father joined the RAF, and my mother and I went to stay with her mother in Dehradun, while my father found himself in a tent on the outskirts of Delhi.

It took two or three days by train from Jamnagar to Dehradun, but trains were not quite as crowded then as they are today and, provided no one got sick, a long train journey was something of an extended picnic, with halts at quaint little stations, railway meals in abundance brought by waiters in smart uniforms, an ever-changing landscape, bridges over mighty rivers, forest, desert, farmland, everything sun-drenched, the air clear and unpolluted except when dust storms swept across the plains. Bottled drinks were a rarity then, the occasional lemonade or 'Vimto' being the only aerated soft drink, apart from soda water which was always available for whisky-pegs. We made our own orange juice or lime juice, and took it with us.

By journey's end we were wilting and soot-covered, but Dehra's bracing winter climate soon brought us back to life.

Scarlet poinsettia leaves and trailing bougainvillaea adorned the garden walls, while in the compounds grew mangoes, lichis, papayas, guavas, and lemons large and small. It was a popular place for retiring Anglo-Indians, and my maternal grandfather, after retiring from the Railways, had built a neat, compact bungalow on Old Survey Road. There it stands today, unchanged except in ownership. Dehra was a small, quiet, garden town, only parts of which are still recognisable now, forty years after I first saw it.

I remember waking in the train early one morning, and looking out of the window at heavy forest trees of every description but mostly sal and shisharm; here and there a forest glade, or a stream of clear water—quite different from the muddied waters of the streams and rivers we had crossed the previous day. As we passed over a largish river (the Song) we saw a herd of elephants bathing; and leaving the forests of the Siwalik hills, we entered the Doon valley, where fields of rice and flowering mustard stretched away to the foothills.

Outside the station we climbed into a tonga, or pony-trap, and rolled creakingly along quiet roads until we reached my grandmother's house. Grandfather had died a couple of years previously and Grandmother lived alone, except for occasional visits from her married daughters and their families, and from her unmarried but wandering son Ken, who was to turn up from time to time, especially when his funds were low. Granny also had a tenant, Miss Kellner, who occupied a portion of the bungalow.

Miss Kellner had been crippled in a carriage accident in Calcutta when she was a girl, and had been confined to a chair all her adult life. She had been left some money by her parents, and was able to afford an ayah and four stout palanquin-bearers, who carried her about when she wanted the chair moved, and took her for outings in a real sedan-chair or sometimes a rickshaw—she had both. Her hands were deformed and she could scarcely hold a pen, but she managed to play cards quite dexterously and taught me a number of card games, which I have now forgotten. Miss Kellner was the only person with whom I could play cards: she allowed me to cheat.

Granny employed a full-time gardener, a wizened old character named Dhuki (Sad), and I don't remember that he ever laughed or smiled. I'm not sure what deep tragedy dwelt behind those dark eyes (he never spoke about himself, even when questioned) but he was tolerant of me, and talked to me about the flowers and their characteristics.

There were rows and rows of sweet-peas; beds full of phlox and sweet-smelling snapdragons; geraniums on the veranda steps, hollyhocks along the garden wall. Behind the house were the fruit trees, somewhat neglected since my grandfather's death, and it was here that I liked to wander in the afternoons, for the old orchard was dark and private and full of possibilities. I made friends with an old jackfruit tree, in whose trunk was a large hole in which I stored marbles, coins, catapults, and other treasures, much as a crow stores the bright objects it picks up during its peregrinations.

I have never been a great tree-climber, having a tendency to fall off branches, but I liked climbing walls (and still do), and it was not long before I had climbed the wall behind the orchard, to drop into unknown territory and explore the bazaars and by-lanes of Dehra.

11

THE ZIGZAG WALK

Uncle Ken always maintained that the best way to succeed in life was to zigzag. 'If you keep going off in new directions,' he declared, 'you will meet new career opportunities!'

Well, opportunities certainly came Uncle Ken's way, but he was not a success in the sense that Dale Carnegie or Deepak Chopra would have defined a successful man...

In a long life devoted to 'muddling through' with the help of the family, Uncle Ken's many projects had included a chicken farm (rather like the one operated by Ukridge in Wodehouse's *Love Among the Chickens*) and a mineral water bottling project. For this latter enterprise, he bought a thousand soda-water bottles and filled them with sulphur water from the springs five miles from Dehra. It was good stuff, taken in small quantities, but drunk one bottle at a time it proved corrosive—'sulphur and brimstone' as one irate customer described it—and angry buyers demonstrated in front of the house, throwing empty bottles over the wall into Grandmother's garden.

Grandmother was furious—more with Uncle Ken than with the demonstrators—and made him give everyone's money back.

'You have to be healthy and strong to take sulphur water,' he explained later.

'I thought it was supposed to make you healthy and strong,' I said.

Grandfather remarked that it did not compare with plain soda-water, which he took with his whisky. 'Why don't you just bottle soda-water?' he said. 'There's a much bigger demand for it.'

But Uncle Ken believed that he had to be original in all things.

'The secret to success is to zigzag,' he said.

'You certainly zigzagged round the garden when your customers were throwing their bottles back at you,' said Grandmother.

Uncle Ken also invented the zigzag walk.

The only way you could really come to know a place well, was to walk in a truly haphazard way. To make a zigzag walk you take the first turning to the left, the first to the right, then the first to the left and so on. It can be quite fascinating provided you are in no hurry to reach your destination. The trouble was that Uncle Ken used this zigzag method even when he had a train to catch.

When Grandmother asked him to go to the station to meet Aunt Mabel who was arriving from Lucknow, he zigzagged through town, taking in the botanical gardens in the west and the limestone factories to the east, finally reaching the station by way of the goods yard, in order, as he said, 'to take it by surprise'.

Nobody was surprised, least of all Aunt Mabel who had taken a tonga and reached the house while Uncle Ken was still sitting on the station platform, waiting for the next train to come in. I was sent to fetch him.

'Let's zigzag home again,' he said.

'Only on one condition, we eat chaat every fifteen minutes,' I said.

So we went home by way of all the most winding bazaars, and in north-Indian towns they do tend to zigzag, stopping at numerous chaat and halwai shops, until Uncle Ken had finished his money. We got home very late and were scolded by everyone; but as Uncle Ken told me, we were pioneers and had to expect to be misunderstood and even maligned. Posterity would recognise the true value of zigzagging.

'The zigzag way,' he said, 'is the diagonal between heart and reason.'

In our more troubled times, had he taken to preaching on the subject, he might have acquired a large following of dropouts. But Uncle Ken was the original dropout. He would not have tolerated others.

Had he been a space traveller he would have gone from star to star, zigzagging across the Milky Way.

Uncle Ken would not have succeeded in getting anywhere very fast, but I think he did succeed in getting at least one convert (myself) to see his point: 'When you zigzag, you are not choosing what to see in this world but you are giving the world a chance to see you!'

12

A BICYCLE RIDE WITH UNCLE KEN

Kissing a girl while sharing a bicycle with her is no easy task, but I managed it when I was thirteen and my cousin Elsa was fourteen. Of course we both fell off in the process, and landed in one of Granny's flowerbeds where we were well cushioned by her nasturtiums.

I was a clumsy boy, always falling off bicycles and cousin Elsa was teaching me to ride properly, making me sit on the front seat while she guided the infernal machine from the carrier seat. The kiss was purely experimental. I had not kissed a girl before and as cousin Elsa seemed eminently kissable, I though I'd start with her. I waited until we were stationary and she was instructing me on the intricacies of the cycle chain, when I gave her a hurried peck on the cheek. She was so startled that she fell backwards taking me and the bicycle with her.

Later, she reported me to Granny, who said, 'We'll have to keep an eye on that boy. He's showing signs of a dissolute nature.'

'What's dissolute, Uncle Ken?' I asked my favourite uncle.

'It means you're going to the dogs. You're not supposed to kiss your cousin.'

'Can I kiss other girls?'

'Only if they are willing.'

'Did you ever kiss a girl, Uncle Ken?'

Uncle Ken blushed. 'Er...well...a long time ago.'

'Tell me about it.'

'Another time.'

'No, tell me now. How old were you?'

'About twenty.'

'And how old was she?'

'A bit younger.'

'And what happened?'

'We went cycling together. I was staying in Agra, where your grandfather worked in the Railways. Daisy's father was an engine-driver. But she didn't like engines, they left her covered with soot. Everyone had a bicycle in those days, only the very rich had cars. And the cars could not keep up with the bicycles. We lived in the cantonment area, where the roads were straight and wide. Daisy and I went on cycle rides to Fatehpur-Sikri and Secunderabad and of course the Taj Mahal, and one evening we saw the Taj Mahal by moonlight and it made us very romantic and when I saw her home we kissed under the Asoka trees.'

'I didn't know you were so romantic, Uncle Ken. Why didn't you marry Daisy?'

'I didn't have a job. She said she'd wait until I got one, but after two years she got tired of waiting. She married a ticket-inspector.'

'Such a sad story,' I said. 'And you still don't have a job.'

Uncle Ken had been through various jobs—private tutor, salesman, shop assistant, hotel manager (until he brought about the closure of the hotel) and cricket coach, this last on the strength of bearing a close resemblance to Geoff Boycott—but at present he was unemployed and only too ready to put his vast experience of life at my disposal.

Not only did he teach me to ride a bicycle, he accompanied me on cycle rides around Dehra and along the lanes and country roads outside the town.

A bicycle provides its rider with a great amount of freedom. A car will take you further but the fact that you're sitting in a confined space takes away from the freedom of the open spaces and unfamiliar roads. On a cycle you can feel the breeze on your face, smell the mango trees in blossom, slow down and gaze at the buffaloes wading in their ponds, or just stop anywhere and get down and enjoy a cup of tea or a glass of sugarcane juice. Foot-slogging takes time and cars are too fast—everything whizzes past you before you can take a second look—and car drivers hate having to stop, they are intent only on reaching their destinations in good time. But a bicycle is just right for someone who likes to take a leisurely look at the world as well as to give the world a chance to look at him.

Uncle Ken and I had some exhilarating bicycle rides during my winter holidays and the most memorable of those was our unplanned visit to a certain rest home situated on the outskirts of the town. It isn't there now so don't go looking for it. We had cycled quite far that day and were tired and thirsty. There was no sign of a tea shop on that particular road but when we arrived at the open gate of an impressive building with a signboard saying 'Rest and Recuperation Centre', we presumed it was a hotel or hostel of sorts and rode straight into the premises. There was an extensive lawn to one side, surrounded by neat hedges and flowering shrubs. A number of people were strolling about the lawn; some were sitting on benches; one or two were straddling a wall, talking to themselves; another was standing alone, singing to a non-existent audience. Some were Europeans and a few were Indians.

We left our cycles in the porch and went in search of refreshments. A lady in a white sari gave us cool water from a sohrai and told us we could wait on a bench just outside their office. But Uncle Ken said we'd prefer to meet some of the guests and led me across the lawn to where the singer was practicing his notes. He was a florid gentleman, heavily built.

'Do you like my singing?' he asked, as we came up.

'Wonderful!' exclaimed Uncle Ken. 'You sing like Caruso.'

'I am Caruso!' affirmed the tenor and let rip the opening notes of a famous operatic aria.

We hurried on and met an elegant couple who were parading up and down the lawn, waving their hands to an invisible crowd.

'Good-day to you, gentlemen,' said a flamboyant individual. 'You're the ambassadors from Sweden, I suppose.'

'If you so wish,' said Uncle Ken gallantly. 'And I have the honour of speaking to—?'

'The Emperor Napoleon, of course.'

'Of course. And this must be the Empress Josephine.' Uncle Ken bowed to the lady beside him.

'Actually, she's Marie Waleska,' said Napoleon. 'Josephine is indisposed today.'

I was beginning to feel like Alice at the Mad Hatter's tea party and began tugging at Uncle Ken's coat-sleeve, whispering that we were getting late for lunch.

A turbaned warrior with a tremendous moustache loomed in front of us. 'I'm Prithviraj Chauhan,' he announced. 'And I invite you to dinner at my palace.'

'Everyone's royalty here,' observed Uncle Ken. 'It's such a privilege to be with you.'

'Me too,' I put in nervously.

'Come with me boy, and I'll introduce you to the others.' Prithviraj Chauhan took me by the hand and began guiding me across the lawn. 'There are many famous men and women here. That's Marco Polo over there. He's just back from China. And if you don't care for Caruso's singing, there's Tansen under that tamarind tree. Tamarind leaves are good for the voice, you know that of course, and that fashionable gentleman there, he's Lord Curzon, who used to be a Viceroy. He's talking to the Sultan of Marrakesh. Come along, I'll introduce you to them... You're the young prince of Denmark, aren't you?'

Before I could refute any claims to royalty, we were intercepted by a white-coated gentleman accompanied by a white-coated assistant. They looked as though they were in charge.

'And what are you doing here, young man?' asked the senior of the two.

'I am with my uncle,' I said, gesturing towards Uncle Ken, who approached and gave the in-charge an affable handshake.

'And you must be Dr Freud,' said Uncle Ken. 'I must say this is a jolly sort of place.'

'Actually, I'm Dr Goel. You must be the new patient we were expecting. But they should have sent you over with someone a little older. Never mind, come along to the office and we'll have you admitted.'

Uncle Ken and I both protested that we were not potential patients but that we had entered the grounds by mistake. We had our bicycles to prove it! However, Dr Goel was having nothing of this deception. He and his assistant linked arms with Uncle Ken and marched him off to the office, while I trailed behind, wondering if I should get on my bicycle and rush back to Granny with the terrible news that Uncle Ken had been incarcerated in a lunatic asylum.

Just then an ambulance arrived with the real patient, a school principal suffering from a persecution complex. He kept shouting that he was perfectly sane, and that his entire staff had plotted to have him put away. This might well have been true, as the staff was there in force to make sure he did not escape.

Dr Goel apologised to Uncle Ken. Uncle Ken apologised to Dr Goel. The good doctor even accompanied us to the gate. He shook hands with Uncle Ken and said, 'I have a feeling we'll see you here again.' He looked hard at my uncle and added, 'I think I've seen you before, sir. What did you say your name was?'

'Geoff Boycott,' said Uncle Ken mischievously, and rode away before they changed their minds and kept him in there.

13

AT SEA WITH UNCLE KEN

With Uncle Ken you had always to expect the unexpected. Even in the most normal circumstances, something unusual would happen to him and to those around him. He was a catalyst for confusion.

My mother should have known better than to ask him to accompany me to England, the year after I'd finished school. She felt that a boy of sixteen was a little too young to make the voyage on his own; I might get lost or lose my money or fall overboard or catch some dreadful disease. She should have realised that Uncle Ken, her only brother (well spoilt by his five sisters), was more likely to do all these things.

Anyway, he was put in charge of me and instructed to deliver me safely to my aunt in England, after which he could either stay there or return to India, whichever he preferred.

Granny had paid for his ticket so in effect he was getting a free holiday which included a voyage on a posh P&O liner.

Our train journey to Bombay passed off without incident, although Uncle Ken did manage to misplace his spectacles, getting down at the station wearing someone else's. This left him a little short-sighted, which might have accounted for his mistaking the stationmaster for a porter and instructing him to look after our luggage.

We had two days in Bombay before boarding the *S.S Strathnaver* and Uncle Ken vowed that we would enjoy ourselves. However, he was a little constrained by his budget and took me to a rather seedy hotel on Lamington Road, where we had to share a toilet with over twenty other people.

'Never mind,' he said. 'We won't spend much time in this dump.' So he took me to Marine Drive and the Gateway of India and to an Irani restaurant in Colaba where we enjoyed a super dinner of curried prawns and scented rice. I don't know if it was the curry, the prawns, or the scent but Uncle Ken was up all night, running back and forth to that toilet, so that no one else had a chance to use it. Several dispirited travellers simply opened their windows and ejected into space, cursing Uncle Ken all the while.

He had recovered by morning and proposed a trip to the Elephanta Caves. After a breakfast of fish pickle, Malabar chilli chutney and sweet Gujarati puris, we got into a launch, accompanied by several other tourists and set off on our short cruise. The sea was rather choppy and we hadn't gone far before Uncle Ken decided to share his breakfast with the fishes of the sea. He was as green as seaweed by the time we went ashore. Uncle Ken collapsed on the sand and refused to move, so we didn't see much of the caves. I brought him some coconut water and he revived a bit and suggested we go on a fast until it was time to board our ship.

We were safely on board the following morning, and the ship sailed majestically out from Ballard Pier, Bombay and India receded into the distance, quite possibly forever as I wasn't sure that I would ever return. The sea fascinated me and I remained on deck all day, gazing at small crafts, passing steamers, sea-birds, the distant shore-line, salt-water smells, the surge of the waves and of course my fellow passengers. I could well understand the fascination it held for writers such as Conrad, Stevenson, Maugham and others.

Uncle Ken, however, remained confined to his cabin. The rolling of the ship made him feel extremely ill. If he had been looking green in Bombay, he was looking yellow at sea. I took my meals in the dining saloon, where I struck up an acquaintance with a well-known palmist and fortune-teller who was on his way to London to make his fortune. He looked at my hand and told me I'd never be rich, but that I'd help other people get rich!

When Uncle Ken felt better (on the third day of the voyage), he struggled up on the deck, took a large lungful of sea air and subsided into a deck-chair. He dozed the day away, but was suddenly wide awake when an attractive blonde strode past us on her way to the lounge. After some time we heard the tinkling of a piano. Intrigued, Uncle Ken rose and staggered into the lounge. The girl was at the piano, playing something classical which wasn't something that Uncle Ken normally enjoyed, but he was smitten by the girl's good looks and he stood enraptured, his eyes brightly gleaming, his jaw sagging. With his nose pressed against the glass of the lounge door, he reminded me of a goldfish who had fallen in love with an angel fish that had just been introduced into the tank.

'What is she playing?' he whispered, aware that I had grown up on my father's classical record collection.

'Rachmaninoff,' I made a guess, 'Or maybe Rimsky Korsakov.'

'Something easier to pronounce,' he begged.

'Chopin,' I said.

'And what's his most famous composition?'

'*Polonaise in E flat*. Or may be it's E minor.'

He pushed open the lounge door, walked in, and when the girl had finished playing, applauded loudly. She acknowledged his applause with a smile and then went on to play something else. When she had finished he clapped again and said, 'Wonderful! Chopin never sounded better!'

'Actually, it's Tchaikovsky,' said the girl. But she didn't seem to mind.

Uncle Ken would turn up at all her practice sessions and very soon they were strolling the decks together. She was Australian, on her way to London to pursue a musical career as a concert pianist. I don't know what she saw in Uncle Ken, but he knew all the right people. And he was quite good-looking in an effete sort of way.

Left to my own devices, I followed my fortune-telling friend around and watched him study the palms of our fellow passengers. He foretold romance, travel, success, happiness, health, wealth, and longevity, but never predicted anything that might upset anyone. As he did not charge anything (he was, after all, on holiday) he proved to be a popular passenger throughout the voyage. Later he was to become quite famous as a palmist and mind-reader, an Indian 'Cheiro', much in demand in the capitals of Europe.

The voyage lasted eighteen days, with stops for passengers and cargo at Aden, Port Said and Marseilles, in that order. It was at Port Said that Uncle Ken and his friend went ashore, to look at the sights and do some shopping.

'You stay on the ship,' Uncle Ken told me. 'Port Said isn't safe for young boys.'

He wanted the girl all to himself, of course. He couldn't have shown off with me around. His 'man of the world' manner would not have been very convincing in my presence.

The ship was due to sail again that evening and passengers had to be back on board an hour before departure. The hours passed easily enough for me as the little library kept me engrossed. If there are books around, I am never bored. Towards evening I went up on deck and saw Uncle Ken's friend coming up the gangway; but of Uncle Ken there was no sign.

'Where's Uncle?' I asked her.

'Hasn't he returned? We got separated in a busy marketplace and I thought he'd get here before me.'

We stood at the railings and looked up and down the pier, expecting to see Uncle Ken among the other returning passengers. But he did not turn up.

'I suppose he's looking for you,' I said. 'He'll miss the boat if he doesn't hurry.'

The ship's hooter sounded. 'All aboard!' called the captain on his megaphone. The big ship moved slowly out of the harbour. We were on our way! In the distance I saw a figure that looked like Uncle Ken running along the pier, frantically waving his arms. But there was no turning back.

A few days later my aunt met me at Tilbury Dock.

'Where's your Uncle Ken?' she asked.

'He stayed behind at Port Said. He went ashore and didn't get back in time.'

'Just like Ken. And I don't suppose he has much money with him. Well, if he gets in touch we'll send him a postal order.'

But Uncle Ken failed to get in touch. He was a topic of discussion for several days, while I settled down in my aunt's house and looked for a job. At sixteen I was working in an office, earning a modest salary and contributing towards my aunt's housekeeping expenses. There was no time to worry about Uncle Ken's whereabouts.

My readers know that I longed to return to India, but it was nearly four years before that became possible. Finally I did come home and as the train drew into Dehra's little station, I looked out of the window and saw a familiar figure on the platform. It was Uncle Ken!

He made no reference to his disappearance at Port Said, and greeted me as though we had last seen each other the previous day.

'I've hired a cycle for you,' he said. 'Feel like a ride?'

'Let me get home first, Uncle Ken. I've got all this luggage.'

The luggage was piled into a tonga, I sat on top of everything and we went clip-clopping down an avenue of familiar lichi trees (all gone now, I fear). Uncle Ken rode behind the tonga, whistling cheerfully.

'When did you get back to Dehra?' I asked.

'Oh, a couple of years ago. Sorry I missed the boat. Was the girl upset?'

'She said she'd never forgive you.'

'Oh well, I expect she's better off without me. Fine piano player. Chopin and all that stuff.'

'Did Granny send you the money to come home?'

'No, I had to take a job working as a waiter in a Greek restaurant. Then I took tourists to look at the pyramids. I'm an expert on pyramids now. Great place, Egypt. But I had to leave when they found I had no papers or permit. They put me on a boat to Aden. Stayed in Aden six months teaching English to the son of a Shiekh. Shiekh's son went to England, I came back to India.'

'And what are you doing now, Uncle Ken?'

'Thinking of starting a poultry farm. Lots of space behind your Gran's house. Maybe you can help with it.'

'I couldn't save much money, Uncle.'

'We'll start in a small way. There is a big demand for eggs, you know. Everyone's into eggs—scrambled, fried, poached, boiled. Egg curry for lunch. Omelettes for dinner. Egg sandwiches for tea. How do you like your egg?'

'Fried,' I said. 'Sunny side up.'

'We shall have fried eggs for breakfast. Funny side up!'

The poultry farm never did happen, but it was good to be back in Dehra, with the prospect of limitless bicycle rides with Uncle Ken.

14

TRAVELS WITH MY BANK MANAGER

1

You couldn't ask for a livelier or more interesting companion than Ohri, my former bank manager. I say 'former', not because he is no longer with us, but because he has gone on to bigger and better things in Mumbai and Dubai where, I am given to understand, the streets are paved with gold. When I knew him he was a wildlife enthusiast with his heart in Corbett country and the Himalayan foothills.

Ohri liked travelling by road, preferably at dawn, the drive punctuated by halts to gaze at peacocks, nilghav, jackals and porcupines.

I'd accompany him occasionally, and one crisp winter morning we got into his battered old Fiat for a leisurely drive from Delhi to Dehradun. But Ohri had no intention of keeping to the main highway or doing anything in a leisurely manner.

'From Roorkee we'll take the Haridwar road, then take a diversion and get onto the forest road through the Rajaji Sanctuary. We'll come out near the Mohand Pass. It is only about fifteen miles. Beautiful forest, lots of wildlife, tigers, herds of elephants, perfectly safe!'

'If you say so,' I said, not having much choice once he was behind the wheel.

By the time we had made it to the Rajaji forest road, dusk had fallen and the peahens were stridently calling up their mates.

There was three raos (dry river beds) to cross on the way to the pass, and at the first of these the front door threatened to come off its hinges.

'Hang on to it!' urged Ohri. 'Keep it from falling off!'

I had an old football scarf with me—a gift from travel writer Bill Aitken, a fellow fan of bottom of the Scottish League club, Alloa Athletic—and I tied this to the door handle, making it easier for me to keep the door from falling open.

Ohri stopped the car and pointed enthusiastically at several hefty dung-cakes in the middle of the road.

'Look, elephant dung!' he cried. 'Maybe we'll be lucky and see some wild elephants.'

'I'm quite content just viewing their leavings,' I said.

'Very good for making paper,' observed Ohri.

'Well, perhaps you could persuade the Reserve Bank to use the stuff for making notes, the large denominations.'

Undeterred by my sarcasm, Ohri started up and drove merrily into the second boulder-strewn rao. A bump, a bang, and we had a flat tyre.

'We'll soon fix it,' said Ohri. 'Will you get the spare tyre out of the dickey?'

Fortunately my struggle with the door prevented me from getting out, because just then a number of wild boars appeared at the side of the road. They had been in search of a little water in the rao and had now stopped in order to take a growing interest in the car and its occupants.

'Better wait until they've gone,' said Ohri. 'Wild boars can be dangerous. Even a tiger will run from a charging boar. Don't let the door fall off!'

I hung onto the door for dear life. I wasn't about to run like a tiger.

We waited. The boars waited.

'Would you like a drink?' asked Ohri after some time. 'There's a bottle here somewhere.'

He produced a full bottle of strong army rum and we took swigs in turn. The boars came a little nearer.

'If we're going to be here all night let's play Under a Scotsman's Kilt,' I suggested. 'I learnt it at school.'

'I didn't know you were gay.'

'I'm not. I'm serious. You give me the first line of a song or poem, and I'll come in with the line "Under aScotman's Kilt." It's great fun. Don't think too hard. The first song that comes to mind...'

'Old Macdonald had a farm.'
'Under a Scotsman's kilt.'
'I wandered lonely as a cloud.'
'Under a Scotsman's kilt.'
'Tiger, tiger burning bright.'
'Under a Scotsman's kilt.'

We continued in this scatological vein for some time until, fortunately for our sanity, the silence of the night was broken by the roar of an approaching motor-cycle. To our amazement, two middle-aged Sikh gentlemen materialised in front of our headlights. The wild boars scattered and vanished into the night.

Our rescuers were in the habit of using the forest road as a short-cut to their farm in the Terai.

Elephants and wild boars did not faze them. They helped us change the tyre, and then they helped us finish the bottle of rum. They even offered to get us another bottle, courtesy a helpful forest guard; but we thanked them profusely and said we had to be on our way. Ohri's wife was waiting for him in Dehradun, rolling pin at the ready. She would flatten him out along with the atta.

Ohri negotiated the remainder of the second rao and then, at the rao before Mohand, the door finally fell off, taking my Scottish football scarf with it.

Ever loyal to Alloa Athletic, I retrieved the scarf, but Ohri left the door behind in the river-bed.

'We'll come back for it another day,' he vowed. I was sure he had another treat in store for me.

2

The next time we met, a few weeks later, Ohri had a new car, one of the latest Marutis.

'Come on, I'll take you for a spin down Tehri Road,' he said. 'We'll be back in time for lunch.'

'Are you sure?' I asked. 'I don't want to miss my afternoon siesta.'

'Nothing better than a nap under a chestnut tree,' said Ohri.

'The last time I slept under a chestnut tree, the langurs kept dropping chestnuts on my head. And this is October and the chestnuts are ready.'

'We'll go no further than Suakholi,' promised Ohri.

And so we set off in his new car, and on the way Ohri told me how he was having an ulcer problem and that Dr Bhist had told him to keep eating biscuits between meals. Apparently the biscuits soaked up the excess acid. On the seat between us I found three packets of biscuits—glucose, cream crackers and a third variety which I did not recognise.

'And what are these?' I asked.

'Dog biscuits,' he said.

'You're eating dog biscuits for your ulcer?'

'No, of course not. We have a dog now, a Labrador. My wife told me to bring home some dog biscuits.'

Ohri kept munching biscuits on the way to Suakholi, where we stopped for tea and more biscuits. 'Do we go home now?' I asked.

'Just a little further,' he urged. 'Don't you want to see the phosphate mines?'

I said I had no particular interest in phosphate mines, but he said we were sure to see some pheasants along the way, and so I let him talk me into an extension of the drive. A little way after Suakholi, we took a turning to the right, and continued along a rough dirt road which was obviously resented by the springs of Ohri's new car. We passed the phosphate mines, which appeared to have been shut down, and continued through a path of mixed forest in the general direction of the next mountain.

'This is not the way home,' I remarked.

'There's a forest rest house around the next bend,' said Ohri. 'Maybe the chowkidar can prepare some lunch for us.'

There was indeed a rest house around the bend, but it looked as though it hadn't been occupied for years. Most of the roof was missing. A wildcat spat at us from a broken wall. There was no sign of a chowkidar or any other human being.

'We'd better go back,' said Ohri. We shared the cream crackers and washed them down with mineral water. Ohri hadn't brought any rum along this time, which was just as well. He hadn't brought enough petrol, either. We hadn't gone very far when the over-taxed car spluttered to a stop.

'We should have turned back from Suakholi,' he said accusingly, as though it was all my fault.

'Well, you might get some in Suakholi,' I said. 'Ask a passing truck-driver. I'll stay here with the car.'

So Ohri trudged up to Suakholi, while I settled down in the shade of a whispering pine and enjoyed my afternoon siesta. When I woke up, it was evening and I was feeling hungry. I went to the car and through the window-glass saw that there were still some biscuits on the front seat. But Ohri had locked all the doors! I returned to the rest house and explored the ruins. There was nothing there that I could eat, except for some wild sorrel growing in the cracks of the building.

Ohri came back just as it was getting dark. He'd brought the petrol but had neglected to bring any food.

On our way back we ate the dog biscuits.

Try them sometime. They are really quite nourishing. And they don't taste too bad if you're really hungry.

When Ohri's wife scolded him for not bringing the dog biscuits, all he could say was, 'Ruskin ate them.'

3

Banks are not normally exciting places, except when there's a bank robbery. But with Ohri around there was never a dull moment.

Our small branch is now computerised, but a few years ago it did not even have a typewriter. They used to borrow mine. Not everyday, but once a year, for a week or two, when their auditors came around.

I had three typewriters—a heavy Godrej, an old Olympic (which I still use occasionally) and an ancient German machine gifted to me by Goel, who is Swiss. The bank's chaprassi would walk down to my place, collect the Godrej, and struggle back up the hill with it. I did not share my Olympic with the bank. But on one occasion, while I was out, the chaprassi took the German machine by mistake and this led to some confusion.

On German typewriters the letter 'Z' occurs where there is normally a 'Y' on an English machine, and if you are not used to it, and are typing fast, you are apt to produce a certain amount of gibberish. If you want to say 'You might pick up yellow fever in Zanzibar', it could come out 'Zou might pick up yellow fever in Yanyibar'! The auditors and my friends at the bank got into many a tangle: zeros became yeros and even euros, Japanese yens became zens. Chinese yuans became zuans. The foreign exchange section was in a fine mess.

It was after this that the bank was hurriedly computerised.

Ohri had left by then. As a last treat he took me along on a nocturnal excursion to see a black panther which, he said, was on the prowl in the vicinity of Barlowganj.

'Black panthers are very rare now,' he told me. 'No one has seen one here in over fifty years.'

'Not since General Barlow shot the last one,' I added rather mischievously.

'We'll go down to Barlowganj tonight,' he said, as enthusiastic as ever. 'We'll sit up for it until dawn.'

'Don't forget the dog biscuits,' I said, 'I get hungry around midnight.'

Biscuits were not required. Mrs Ohri gave us a substantial dinner, guaranteed to put me to sleep while Ohri sat up looking for his black panther.

'It's just a big black dog,' she told me. 'The chowkidar at St George's school has a Bhotia mastiff. At night it gets mistaken for a panther.'

This wasn't going to deter Ohri from driving us down to the valley and back again, with numerous stops for panther-watching and swigs of rum. The stars looked down from a clear night sky. Ohri waxed poetic, 'The night has a thousand eyes—'

'Under a Scotsman's kilt,' I put in.

'Shh...we mustn't talk too much. We'll frighten it away.'

'If you see a panther, don't anther,' I quoted Ogden Nash.

Ohri complained that I wasn't taking the expedition seriously, so I closed my eyes and fell asleep. Presently I was awake again. He was shaking me, whispering urgently—'Look, there's something in those bushes, you can see them moving!'

They were indeed moving, and soon parted to reveal an elderly villager who had got up early in order to relieve himself in the great outdoors. He was not pleased at having his privacy disturbed.

'Have you seen a panther?' asked Ohri. 'Kala baghera?'

'Baghera yourself,' snapped the villager, who seemed equally at home in Hindi and English. 'Can't have a decent—in peace. Tourists all over the place,' and he stomped off into the darkness.

We were home before dawn. Mrs Ohri gave us a splendid breakfast.

'Did you see anything?' she asked.

'Too many people about,' I said. 'No room left for leopards, black or spotted.'

'We heard it,' insisted Ohri. 'I heard it growling in the bushes.'

'How do you know it was a black panther?' asked Mrs Ohri. 'It may have been spotted.'

'Not only that,' I added, 'it was carrying an empty mineral water bottle in lieu of a lota!'

15

GRANNY'S TREE-CLIMBING

Granny was a genius. You'd like to know why?
Because she could climb trees. Spreading or high,
She'd be up their branches in a trice. And mind you,
When last she climbed a tree she was sixty-two.

Ever since childhood, she'd had this gift
For being happier in a tree than in a lift;
And though, as time went by, she would be told
That climbing trees should stop when one grew old—
And that growing old should be gone about gracefully—
She'd laugh and say, 'Well, I'll grow old disgracefully!
I can do it better.' And we had to agree;
For in all the garden there wasn't a tree
She hadn't been up at one time or another—

(Having learned to climb from a loving brother
When she was six)—but it was feared by all
That one day she'd suffer a terrible fall.

The outcome was different—while we were in town
She climbed a tree and couldn't come down!
She remained on her perch until we came home,
We fetched her a ladder, and she came down alone.

As she looked a bit shaken, we sent for our doc,
Who said, 'She is fine—just a bit of a shock.'
He took Granny's temperature. 'Some fever,' he said;
'I strongly recommend a quiet week in bed.'

We sighed with relief and tucked her up well—
Poor Granny! It was just like a season in hell;
Confined to her bedroom, while every breeze
Murmured of summer and dancing leaves....
But she held her peace till she felt stronger,
Then sat up and said, 'I'll lie here no longer!'
She called for my father and told him undaunted
That a house in a tree-top was what she now wanted.
My Dad knew his duty. He said, 'That's all right—
'You'll have what you want—I shall start work tonight.'

With my expert assistance, he soon finished the chore,
Made her a tree-house with windows and a door.

So Granny moved up; and now, everyday,
I go to her room with glasses and a tray.
She sits there in state and drinks cocktails with me,
Upholding her right to reside in a tree.

    [Written for Grandmothers' Rights Everywhere]

16

MY FAILED OMELETTES —AND OTHER DISASTERS

In nearly fifty years of writing for a living, I have never succeeded in writing a best-seller. And now I know why. I can't cook. Had I been able to do so, I could have turned out a few of those sumptuous looking cookery books that brighten up the bookstore windows before being snapped up by folk who can't cook either.

As it is, if I were forced to write a cook book, it would probably be called *Fifty Different Ways of Boiling an Egg, and Other Disasters*.

I used to think that boiling an egg would be a simple undertaking. But when I came to live at 7,000 feet in the Himalayan foothills, I found that just getting the water to boil was something of an achievement. I don't know if it's the altitude or the density of the water, but it just won't come to the boil in time for breakfast. As a result my eggs are only half-boiled. 'Never mind,' I tell everyone; 'half-boiled eggs are more nutritious than full-boiled eggs.'

'Why boil them at all?' asks Gautam, who is my Mr Dick, always offering good advice. 'Raw eggs are probably healthier.'

'Just you wait and see,' I told him. 'I'll make you a cheese omelette you'll never forget.' And I did. It was a bit messy, as I was over-generous with the tomatoes, but I thought it tasted rather good. Gautam, however, pushed his plate away, saying, 'You forgot to put in the egg.'

101 Failed Omelettes might well be the title of my best-seller.

I love watching other people cook—a habit that I acquired at a young age, when I would watch my granny at work in the kitchen, turning out delicious curries, koftas and custards. I would try helping her, but she soon put a stop to my feeble contributions. On one occasion, she asked me to add a cup of spices to a large curry dish she was preparing, and absent-mindedly I added a cup of sugar. The result—a very sweet curry! Another invention of mine.

I was better at remembering Granny's kitchen proverbs. Here are some of them:

'There is skill in all things, even in making porridge.'

'Dry bread at home is better then curried prawns abroad.'

'Eating and drinking should not keep men from thinking.'

'Better a small fish than an empty dish.'

And her favourite maxim, with which she reprimanded me whenever I showed signs of gluttony: 'Don't let your tongue cut your throat.'

MY FAILED OMELETTES—AND OTHER DISASTERS 107

And as for making porridge, it's certainly no simple matter. I made one or two attempts, but it always came out lumpy.

'What's this?' asked Gautam suspiciously, when I offered him some.

'Porridge!' I said enthusiastically. 'It's eaten by those brave Scottish Highlanders who were always fighting the English!'

'And did they win?' he asked.

'Well—er—not usually. But they were outnumbered!'

He looked doubtfully at the porridge. 'Some other time,' he said.

So why not take the advice of Thoreau and try to simplify life? Simplify, simplify! Or simply sandwiches...

These shouldn't be too difficult, I decided. After all, they are basically bread and butter. But have you tried cutting bread into thin slices? Don't. It's highly dangerous. If you're a pianist, you could be putting your career at great risk.

You must get your bread ready sliced. Butter it generously. Now add your fillings. Cheese, tomato, lettuce, cucumber, whatever. Gosh, I was really going places! Slap another slice of buttered bread over this mouth-watering assemblage. Now cut in two. Result: Everything spills out at the sides and onto the table-cloth.

'Now look what you've gone and done,' says Gautam, in his best Oliver Hardy manner.

'Never mind,' I tell him. 'Practice makes perfect!'

And one of these days you're going to find *Bond's Book of Better Sandwiches* up there on the best-seller lists.

17

A LONG STORY

I live right on top of a hill and Gautam's school is right at the bottom; so I thought it would be a good idea if I walked the two miles to school with him every morning. I would be company for the boy, and the walk, I felt, would do wonders for my sagging waistline.

'Tell me a story,' he said the first time we set off together. And so I told him one. And the next day I told him another. A story a day, told on the long walk through the deodars became routine until I discovered that in this way I was writing myself out—that, story invented and told, I would come home to the realisation that the day's creative work was done and that I couldn't face my desk or typewriter.

So I decided it had to be a serial story. And I found that the best way to keep it going was to invent a man-eating leopard who carried off a different victim every day. An expanding population, I felt, could sustain his depredations over the months and even the years.

Small boys love blood-thirsty man-eaters, and Gautam was no exception. Every day, in the story, one of the townsfolk disappeared, a victim to the leopard's craving for human flesh. He started with the town gossip and worked his way through the clerk who'd lost my file, the barber who'd cut my hair too short, and the shopkeeper who'd sold me the previous year's fireworks, and—well, there's no end to the people who can be visualised as suitable victims.

I must confess that I was getting as much pleasure out of the tale as Gautam. I think Freud might have had a theory or two about my attitude.

'When is it going to be shot?' asked Gautam one morning. 'Not yet,' I said, 'not yet.'

But towards the end of the year I was beginning to have qualms of conscience. Who was I, a mere mortal, to decide on who should be eaten and who should survive? Although the population had been reduced, the accommodation problem remained the same.

Well things came to a head when a real leopard appeared on the hillside and made off with my neighbour's pet pekinese.

Had I, with my fevered imaginings, brought into being an actual leopard? Only a dog-eater, true: but one never knew when it might start on people. And I was still well-fleshed, in spite of the long walks.

So the story had to end.

'The man-eater is dead,' I announced last week.
'Who shot it?'
'It wasn't shot. It just died.'
'Of old age?'
'No. Of ulcerative colitis.'
'What's that?' asked Gautam.
'Acute indigestion,' I said. 'It ate too many people.'

18

GEORGE AND RANJI

When I heard that my cousin George had again escaped from the mental hospital in a neighbouring town, I knew it wouldn't be long before he turned up at my doorstep. It usually happens at the approach of the cricket season. No problem, I thought. I'll just bundle him into a train and take him back to the hospital.

Cousin George had been there, off and on, for a few years. He wasn't the violent type and was given a certain amount of freedom—with the result that he occasionally wandered off by himself, sometimes, to try and take in a Test match. You see, George did not suffer from the delusion that he was Napoleon or Ghengis Khan, he was convinced that he was the great Ranji, prince of cricketers, and that he had just been selected to captain India—quite forgetting that Ranji had actually played for England!

So when George turned up on my front step I wasn't surprised to find him carrying a cricket bat in one hand and a protective box in the other.

'Aren't you ready?' he asked. 'The match starts at eleven.'

'There's plenty of time,' I said, recalling that the train left at eleven-fifteen. 'Why don't you come in and relax while I get ready?'

George sat down and asked for a glass of beer. I brought him one and he promptly emptied it over a pot of ferns.

'They look thirsty,' he said. I dressed hurriedly, anxious to get moving before he started practising his latest cuts on my cutglass decanter. Then, arm in arm, we walked to the gate and hailed an auto rickshaw.

'Railway station,' I whispered to the driver.

'Ferozeshah Kotla,' said George in rising tones, naming Delhi's famous cricket ground. No matter, I thought, I'll straighten out the driver as we go along, I bundled George into the rickshaw and we were soon heading in the direction of Kotla.

'Railway station,' I said again, in tones that could not be denied.

'Kotla,' said cousin George, just as firmly.

The scooter driver kept right on course for the cricket ground. Apparently George had made a better impression on him.

'Look,' I said, tapping the driver on the shoulder. 'This is my cousin and he's not quite right in the head. He's just escaped from a mental asylum and if I'm to get him back there tonight, we must catch the eleven-fifteen train.'

The scooter driver slowed down and looked from cousin George to me and back again. George gave him a winning smile and looking in my direction, tapped his forehead significantly. The driver nodded in sympathy and kept straight on for the stadium.

Well, I've always believed that the dividing line between sanity and insanity is a very thin one, but I had never realised it was quite so thin—too thin for my own comfort! Who was crazy, George, me or the driver?

We had almost reached Kotla and I had no intention of watching over cousin George through a whole day's play. He gets excited at cricket matches—which is strange considering how dull they can be. On one occasion, he broke through the barriers and walked up to the wicket with his bat, determined to bat at Number 3 (Ranji's favourite position, apparently) and assaulted an umpire who tried to escort him from the ground. On another occasion he streaked across the ground, wearing nothing but his protective box.

But it was I who confirmed the driver's worst fears by jumping off the rickshaw as it slowed down, and making my getaway. I've never been able to discover if cousin George had any money with him, or if the rickshaw driver got paid. Rickshaw drivers are inclined at times to be violent, but then so are inmates of mental hospitals. Anyway, George seems to have no memory of the incident.

Three days later, I received word from the hospital that he had returned of his own accord, boasting that he had hit a century—so presumably, he had participated in the match in some form or another.

All's well that ends well, or so I like to think. Cousin George was not usually a violent man, but I have a funny feeling about the rickshaw driver. I never saw him again in Delhi, and unless he has moved elsewhere, I'm afraid his disappearance might well be connected with cousin George's rickshaw ride. After all, the Jamuna is very near Kotla.

19

CRICKET—FIELD PLACINGS

Long leg has a cramp in one leg,
Short leg has a cramp in two;
Twelfth man is fielding at mid-off,
Because mid-on's gone off to the loo.
As short square leg has a long leg,
Long-off has been moved further off;
Silly-point goes back to gully
Cover-point backs off a pace or two.
Everyone is thinking of the drinks' trolley
When first slip lets a catch through his fingers,
Forgetting the old ball is now new.

20

WHATEVER HAPPENED TO ROMANCE?

I hate telephones. That shrill ringing in the middle of the afternoon or late at night is not only nerve-jangling, it means I have to interrupt my reading or writing or sleeping, or my enjoyment of music, or a cricket or football match which is beginning to absorb me. Nothing would induce me to keep a cell phone under my pillow or in my pocket; the landline is bad enough. I usually let someone else answer it.

Gautam does it quite well, except that he sometimes trips up and says, 'Dada is saying he is not at home', or 'Dada is saying, why don't you go to the hell?' A straightforward boy, is Gautam.

Just occasionally I get a nice phone call telling me there is a cheque in the mail but more often than not it is a request for a donation or an invitation to address a conference on Alzheimer's Disease in Ageing Authors, or the Superiority of the Female in Most Insect Species, or Population Growth in the Context of Climate Change. I have every respect for people who lecture, but I have no desire to be one of them or even listen to them. There are better things to do with our time on this earth.

Still, just occasionally it's nice to get a phone call from an old friend, and when that old friend is a girl I knew and loved nearly forty years ago, the heart skips a beat or two, the circulation improves, and suddenly one feels younger and sprightlier and ready for anything.

And so it was the other evening when the phone rang and Gautam picked it up and said, 'Dada, a lady is wanting to talk to you.'

'Does she sound nice?'

'All right. She has a cough, I think.'

I took the phone and said hello.

'Is that Ruskin?'

'It is.'

'I am Sushila.'

'Who?'

'Sushila, don't you remember me? We met in Lodhi Gardens, when I was a girl.'

'Sushila!' I exclaimed. 'Not *my* Sushila?'

'Of course.'

Memories came flooding back. Of Sushila sharing jamuns with me; holding hands when the lights dimmed in the Regal cinema; kissing her hand when I saw her home; meeting her again in a hill-station. Picnics. Romance. More jamuns. More kisses. Would she marry me? She had to think about it...

'Why is your hand trembling?' asks Gautam, watching me as I struggle to articulate on the phone.

'Sushila,' I say again. 'After all these years. How many children do you have now?'

Not a very romantic question, but it had to be asked.

'Six,' she says. 'Two are married. I'm a grandmother.'

'Oh!' I try to visualise Sushila as a grandmother but find it impossible. Will she have a double chin like me? I hope not. She had such sweet dimples.

'It's nice of you to remember me,' I say.

'But you have forgotten me.'

'No, no. I think of you very often.'

'Then do me a favour.'

'Anything you say.'

'Well, it is like this. My sister-in-law, my husband's sister, wants to get her little boy admitted to St George's. She feels you must have influence there.'

'None at all, I'm afraid.'

This wasn't very romantic. It wasn't even exciting. After forty years a former sweetheart rings me up, and instead of saying she still loves me, she asks me to help with a school admission.

'You must know all these school people.'

'Actually, I don't.'

'They must know you, then.'

'Only distantly. In any case, they all conduct admission tests and interviews.'

'You can't help then?'

'I don't see how, unless I do the test myself.'

A pause at the other end of the line. Then: 'Well, it was nice talking to you, Mr Bond.'

'Same here.'

'You must come and see us sometime. The children would love to meet you.'

'Same here. All six of them.'

'And the grandchildren.'

'And the grandchildren.'

End of phone call, end of romance. Down memory lane no more!

'Who was that?' asked Gautam.

'Just an old friend.'

'Old or young friend?'

'Very old. She must have three chins by now.'

Sometimes it's better to forget the more passionate encounters of our youth, especially if they ended in painful partings. And sometimes we would like to forget the recent past, or even the present, if things haven't worked out the way we would have liked.

'Have you any idea who I am?' asked an elderly gentleman, sitting down beside me on a bench opposite the Cambridge

Book Depot. A discarded bus ticket fluttered to the ground, settling near his feet. He was a total stranger, but I am used to being accosted by strangers, especially on the busy Mall Road.

'I'm afraid I don't,' I said, 'perhaps you could tell me.'

'If I knew, I wouldn't be asking you,' he said fretfully. And then, seeing that I was about to move on, he added: 'The trouble is, I've lost my memory.'

'It happens to the best of us. Alzheimer's. Rita Hayworth, Ronald Reagan... actors get it, authors get it. Can you remember how you lost it?'

'If I could remember that, I'd find it again, wouldn't I?'

'I suppose so. If you wanted to...'

'I should think I would.' He spoke excellent English. 'But I don't want to get into an argument about it. I hate arguments of a hypothetical nature. Have you any idea at all who I might be?'

I hadn't realised his memory loss was that bad, but I resolved to help him. Perhaps he was another author.

'Where are you staying?' I asked.

'I haven't a clue. I've been visiting all the hotels for the last two hours, looking through the registers, to see if I could recognise my name—but I haven't had any luck so far. All I can remember is this: I was sitting in the open when a large object moved across the face of the sun, blotting everything out.'

'I don't think we've had an eclipse recently. You don't remember where you were sitting?'

'It may have been outside my hotel room. Unless, of course, I live here permanently—but no one seems to recognise me...I'm afraid it's the sort of memory loss that the Emperor Shah Alam suffered from—very convenient for an emperor, but if I don't recover my memory soon, I won't have anywhere to stay tonight!'

'If you know so much about an emperor's ailments, you might be a historian,' I ventured, in my best Sherlock Holmes manner. 'A professor of history or something like that, definitely an academic.'

He seemed quite pleased. 'Perhaps you're right. All along I've had the feeling that I must be a person of some distinction.'

'You do a lot of writing and desk work,' I observed.

'How do you know?'

'Well, the elbows of your coat are rather worn, and your cuffs slightly frayed. You are wearing your reading glasses instead of distance glasses, having mislaid the latter. Two pens in your coat pocket—you don't use a computer. Yes, a person of distinction, but also a person of limited means—undoubtedly a teacher.'

'But how clever of you!'

'Elementary, my dear Professor Dutt.'

'Dutt! Is that my name? How on earth did you find out?'

'It wasn't very difficult. You see, having determined that you were a college professor, I had only to find out where you came from. Well, from the bus ticket that you threw away when you sat down, I saw that you had come from Karnal. Now I happen to know that there is an excellent college in Karnal, with as many as three professors of history—Professor

Das, Mansaram and Dutt. Professor Das is well-known for his dislike of Western clothes, and as you, sir, are dressed like a British academic, you could not be Das. Nor could you be Professor Mansaram.'

'And why not?'

'Because only last month he suffered a heart attack, and a holiday at this altitude would not be recommended. You must, therefore, be Professor Dutt.'

'He's Dutt, all right,' came a stentorian voice from behind, and I turned, startled, to find a large cauliflower-shaped lady bearing down on us.

Judging from the proprietorial look in her eyes, and the cringing expression in the professor's, the advancing Nemesis was obviously his wife.

'I've been looking for you everywhere,' she snapped.

'I haven't been anywhere,' mumbled the absent-minded professor. 'Anyway, here I am, dear.'

'Did he tell you he'd lost his memory?' asked the good lady. 'He always uses that ploy to gain the sympathy of strangers.'

'He's no stranger,' cried the professor. 'He's a friend of Dr Mansaram!'

Mrs Dutt wasn't impressed. She loomed over her husband like an over-burdened rain-cloud, and all the sunshine went out of the professor's life.

'Goodbye, kind sir,' he called, as she bundled him away.

And as I watched this unhappy marital scene, I wondered if a similar fate might not have befallen me had my proposal to Sushila been accepted, long, long ago.

A sweet girl, but strong-minded too. Would she have grown into someone resembling Mrs Dutt? On the telephone she had sounded quite determined. And I am, after all, an easy-going, tolerant, accommodating person, just a little absent-minded too.

'Goodbye!' I called to Professor Dutt, as he receded into the distance. 'Give my regards to Dr Mansaram!'

You couldn't really blame him for wanting to lose his memory. I might have done the same, given his circumstances.

21

IN PRAISE OF OLDER WOMEN

In the previous chapter I may have given the impression that I am something of a misogynist. This is not the case. While the path of true love and romance proved rather stony, and while I may have faltered at the altar or backed away from the registrar's office, I have always enjoyed the friendship and company of women. Older women, in particular, have always been stimulating, in the nicest sense of the word.

I was only twelve when I was smitten by a girl of eighteen, a kind and beautiful Anglo-Indian girl who broke many hearts before she went on to marry a Sergeant-Major in the British Army. But that was puppy love, and I soon recovered from the condition.

What I really want to do here is to recall some of the women who helped me along the way, or who were simply good companions. If you really want to know what I mean by companionship, you must get hold of J.B. Priestley's classic novel, *The Good Companions*—a wonderful tale of friendship growing out of shared experience, as an incongruous group of eccentric but talented people take to the road performing in little theatres across England.

Well, my own performances are limited to putting words on paper, and occasionally travelling about India, reading and talking to children in numerous schools, where almost all the principals and teachers are women. Having grown up in a boarding school dominated by male teachers who were more interested in getting us on to the sports field, it's refreshing to find schools where the children are encouraged to read and write and not only as a part of their curriculum. In spite of the rival attractions of television and the Internet, the number of book-lovers is on the increase, and this is due largely to the efforts of enlightened schoolteachers—and just occasionally enlightened parents!

Certainly my father encouraged me to read and I wish all fathers would do the same for their children. But when I became a writer, my first editors were women—Diana Athill, who encouraged me to write my first novel, and Kaye Webb, who published my stories in *Young Elizabethan*. Diana became a good friend and helped to make life tolerable for me during those lonely years in London. She was fifteen years older than me, but somehow I never noticed this. We had so much to talk about (books, films, music) and so many places to visit (the theatre, cinemas, restaurants, parks). When, finally, I left

London to return to India, she was the only person I really missed.

★

A woman of similar intellectual attainments, but not as close to me, was Marie Seton, who I knew in Delhi in the early 1960s.

Today, Marie Seton is probably best remembered for her biography of Satyajit Ray. She spent many years studying his cinematic art, knew him personally and was a true enthusiast for his work.

Even before she became a devotee of Ray's work, she had been a film enthusiast, and I'd come across her name when I was a raw youth in London, in 1953. A lonely boy who had grown up on films, I would haunt the small cinemas such as the Academy, off Leicester Square, and the Everyman in Hampstead, taking in everything from silent classics to the lyrical films of Jean Renoir and the comedies of Jacques Tati. There was a season of Eisenstein, I remember. *Battleship Potemkin*, of course. And an edited version of the unfinished *Que Viva Mexico*; edited by a certain Marie Seton, of whom I knew absolutely nothing. But I remembered the name because the film had been memorable and I'd been to see it several times.

Seven years later, when I was living and working in New Delhi, I met the person behind the name. I don't remember how I met her. I was never one for going to parties, and in any case parties were a rarity in Delhi in the 1950s and 1960s. I was working for CARE at the time, and it's possible that

I was introduced to her by Oden Meeker, the Chief of CARE who was an author in his own right. I had written just one novel till then—*The Room on the Roof*—and he would very kindly give it to people he knew and urge them to read it. That's how Marie Seton got a copy. And when, quite by chance, I bumped into her somewhere or the other, she said, 'I've read your book—it's absolutely marvellous!' and when she introduced herself to me as Marie Seton, I was able to say, 'But not as marvellous as your work on *Que Viva Mexico*!'

There's nothing like a little mutual admiration to set off an enduring relationship.

Marie Seton enjoyed a good conversation, provided she did most of the talking. When she found I was a good listener, she would ask me to meet her in the evenings at Nirula's coffee café at Connaught Circus. It was never boring listening to her, but I soon learnt to sit across the table from her because, if I sat beside her, I would get a crick in my neck from having to keep my head turned constantly in her direction.

Apart from her vast knowledge of films, mostly European, she was also well up on all the latest authors, artists and musicians, and seemed to be an expert on the British Royal family. She was not averse to imparting tidbits of scandal in regard to princes and princesses, dukes and duchesses. I loved listening to her gossip, although I must admit that I can't remember much of it now. She also knew several famous film stars and gave me confidential asides on who was gay, who was straight, who was sexless, and the many who were having extra-marital affairs. Gary Cooper, she told me, was the best-hung man in Hollywood; Charlie Chaplin was a sex maniac; Tyrone Power was gay; and ladies' man Errol Flynn really had nothing to write home about.

All the gossip was not without a solid foundation in fact, as I was to find out in time to come. It was Marie who told me that Somerset Maugham had disowned his daughter, that Richard Burton was an alcoholic and that Merle Oberon, the actress, had been born in Calcutta and not in Tasmania as she claimed. All true, of course!

Marie Seton was an independent woman who moved about a good deal, so I was not surprised when, a few months later, I bumped into her on the Mall in Darjeeling.

No time for coffee and gossip because she was busy watching Satyajit Ray make his new film, *Kanchenjunga*.

When Marie spotted me on the road, she called out: 'Have you got my Henry Green?'

'No,' I said, 'I've never read Henry Green.' And haven't done so till this day. But she seemed to think she'd lent me one of his books and continued to press me about it.

When, finally, I'd convinced her that I was not a Henry Green abduct, she took the trouble to introduce me to the great man himself, Satyajit Ray.

Mr Ray was, as always, courteous and friendly and invited me to watch the shooting of some of their outdoor scenes. I did so but couldn't see Marie again as she seemed to be having an affair with a still-photographer.

I was in Darjeeling on business for CARE and was staying at the Everest Hotel, where two film crews were in residence—

Mr Ray and his unit, and Shammi Kapoor and his crew who were working on a film called *Professor*, if my memory serves me right.

These two production units provided a sharp contrast in their approach to filming—Ray making his film entirely on location, the Bollywood lot using the hill-station merely as a backdrop for several song and dance routines, one of them on the railway-tracks! While Ray symbolised the natural in cinematic art, Kapoor and Co. stood for the artificial.

After this encounter, I did not see Marie Seton again. I left Delhi for a somewhat reclusive life in the hills, while she continued with her multifarious activities, especially her excellent biography of Satyajit Ray.

While on the subject of older women who charmed or fascinated me, I cannot forget Lillian, or Lily as we called her, who was some twelve years my senior. Her mother was a friend of my grandmother's and Lily had grown up in Dehradun. She was a pretty, fun-loving girl who at the age of eighteen accepted a proposal of marriage from a British soldier who was stationed in Dehra during World War II. I was invited to be a page-boy at the wedding, my reward being a large slice of wedding-cake, and my duty was to fling endless supplies of confetti on the wedding guests—something I did with great gusto, being only six at the time.

She was given a wonderful wedding cake, tier upon tier of icing, spangled with all sorts of colourful sugary appendages, and within the edifice an assortment of raisins and dried fruits embedded in a scrumptious base. I can still wax poetic about such creations!

As a page-boy I was given an extra large helping, and as a result I was as enthusiastic as anyone in giving Lily and her pink-cheeked soldier boy an enthusiastic send-off.

I am writing about Lily not because I had a crush on her, but because I was to encounter her at various periods of her life and mine, and on each occasion she was married to a different person. In the course of a turbulent life, Lily went through five husbands. I admired her for her resilience, tenacity, and optimism—for she went through life in the hope that she would one day find the perfect man, partner and lover and everything else, and of course there is no such thing, man being a very imperfect creation.

Eleven years after attending Lily's marriage in Dehra, I was in Jersey, in the Channel Islands, where I met her again. The soldier boy had vanished leaving her with a small son. She was now married to a greengrocer, who had given her two strapping daughters. Unfortunately the greengrocer could not live up to Lily's high standards of husbandry and soon began hitting the bottle. If he was too inebriated she would lock him out of the house. On one occasion he climbed up a drainpipe to attempt an entry through a second-floor window. She pushed him out and he landed in some hydrangea bushes and had to be hospitalised. I did not see much of her during this period but got all the inside information from her aunt, who was fond of me and often had me over for meals.

After my return to India, I heard (from the same aunt) that Lily had divorced the greengrocer and left the children with the aunt. She had then proceeded to Rhodesia (now Zimbabwe) where she had married a wealthy white farmer who had two grown sons from his previous marriage, the first wife having succumbed to yellow fever. Lily remained in Rhodesia for three or four years surviving all forms of fever, but finally grew bored with the lonely farm life, and left the land and her husband in order to return to India for a short spell.

This was where I met her again, shortly after her fourth marriage to a former big-game hunter who had now, in his early sixties, taken up fishing. Lily could not get excited about fishing but while dear Frank was away on his trips, she entertained quite lavishly at the old family home, and as an old family friend I was invited to these junkets. Lily would occasionally drop in at my place for a gin and tonic and to talk about old times in Dehra. We joined a few picnic parties—those were the days when picnics were still in vogue—and had some great times. She was a fun-loving person who seemed to have fallen into the bad habit of marrying individuals whose temperaments were totally opposed to hers.

Finally, tiring of the quiet hill-station life, she told Frank he could spend the rest of his life fishing and took off for America, where she worked as a private nurse. She married one of her patients, a wealthy man who lived on a large estate in New Orleans, who was swept away in his wheel-chair when

Hurricane Katrina flooded the city. Hurricane Lily inherited his fortune.

This brief sketch does not do justice to Lily. She deserves an epic novel to herself. And it would have to include her family history, which is equally fascinating. Her grandfather, a British Civil Servant stationed in old Madras, with a wife and children in England, fell in love with a fourteen-year-old Muslim girl and insisted on marrying her. As a result, he had to give up his job and leave Madras. The couple settled in Dehradun, where they started a family of their own. They had two sons and two daughters, and each of the children was given a house in Dehra and Mussoorie, for their father had an independent income. I never saw him because he died before I was born, but I saw his widow when she was an old woman in her late seventies—a tiny little lady with dark smouldering eyes, who must have used them to bewitch the Englishman who had thrown up career, family and social standing in order to marry her.

One of the children (Lily's aunt) had wanted to adopt me when I was a toddler but my parents would not part with me. Had they done so, I might have inherited one of the houses, quite possibly The Parsonage, now owned by my friend Victor Banerjee, the well-known thespian.

Victor is no parson, but we like to call him the Vicar. There is an aura of sanctity around his dwelling, surrounded as it is by sacred deodars, flying squirrels and retired company executives.

★

Someone who did go into a novel—my first—was 'Meena', the older woman with whom young Rusty falls in love in *The Room on the Roof*.

In the novel she is the mother of Kishen, who befriends the runaway Rusty. As many readers have inferred, the novel is autobiographical in essence, and Rusty is the author as a boy. It's true that I was infatuated with Meena (not her real name), who was some fifteen years older than me, the mother of three children, Kishen being the eldest. Her husband, a PWD engineer who had been suspended on a corruption charge, was hitting the bottle in a big way.

Tea and sympathy were the order of the day. Meena gave me tea and I gave her sympathy. She also made wonderful pakoras and I have always believed that the best way to a young man's heart is through his stomach.

Apart from that, she was a beautiful woman, and I was quite smitten, ready to carry out her slightest wish. I ran errands for her, typed out her husband's appeals for reinstatement, gave English lessons to her ten-year-old son and even held the baby when she was busy with other things. This dog-like devotion was rewarded with amusement, affection and even companionship, but she was ever faithful to her husband who seldom emerged from a drunken stupor.

In the novel, Meena dies, killed in a road accident; the alcoholic husband staggers on. This was because of the exigencies of the plot. In reality, it was my friend's father who succumbed to cirrhosis. Meena lived on to a healthy old age.

I did not see her again, but I am told that she remained beautiful into her later years. She had that classical type of Indian beauty, personified in screen stars such as Kamini Kaushal and Nargis, that does not fade with time.

At a book-reading in the Capital not long ago, a student stood up and asked me: 'How could you fall in love with a married woman who was much older than you?'

To which I could only reply: 'I just couldn't help it!'

Meena was not in love with me, that would have been expecting too much; but she was not displeased with my attention. She was like the character in Wilde's *A Woman of No Importance* who says: 'Men always want to be a woman's first love. That is their clumsy vanity. We women have a more subtle instinct about things. What we like is to be a man's last romance.'

And yet it was Meena who set me on the road to romance. For the next ten years I was writing love stories. But in none of them did the lovers live happily every after.

22

WHO KISSED ME IN THE DARK?

This chapter, or story, could not have been written but for a phone call I received last week. I'll come to the caller later. Suffice to say that it triggered off memories of a hilarious fortnight in the autumn of that year (can't remember which one) when India and Pakistan went to war with each other. It did not last long, but there was plenty of excitement in our small town, set off by a rumour that enemy parachutists were landing in force in the ravine below Pari Tibba.

The road to this ravine led past my dwelling, and one afternoon I was amazed to see the town's constabulary, followed by hundreds of concerned citizens (armed mostly with hockey sticks) taking the trail down to the little stream where I usually went bird-watching. The parachutes turned out to be bedsheets from a nearby school, spread out to dry by the dhobis who lived on the opposite hill. After days of incessant rain the sun had come out, and the dhobis had finally got a chance to dry the school bedsheets on the verdant hillside. From afar they did look a bit like open parachutes. In times of crisis, it's wonderful what the imagination will do.

There were also black-outs. It's hard for a hill-station to black itself out, but we did our best. Two or three respectable people were arrested for using their torches to find their way home in the dark. And of course, nothing could be done about the lights on the next mountain, as the people there did not even know there was a war on. They did not have radio or television or even electricity. They used kerosene lamps or lit bonfires!

We had a smart young set in Mussoorie in those days, mostly college students who had also been to convent schools and some of them decided it would be a good idea to put on a show—or old-fashioned theatrical extravaganza—to raise funds for the war effort. And they thought it would be a good idea to rope me in, as I was the only writer living in Mussoorie in those innocent times. I was thirty-one and I had never been a college student but they felt I was the right person to direct a one-act play in English. This was to be the centrepiece of the show.

I forget the name of the play. It was one of those drawing-room situation comedies popular from the 1920s, inspired by such successes as *Charley's Aunt* and *Tons of Money*. Anyway, we went into morning rehearsals at Hakman's, one of the older hotels, where there was a proper stage and a hall large enough to seat at least two hundred spectators.

The participants were full of enthusiasm, and rehearsals went along quite smoothly. They were an engaging bunch of young people—Guttoo, the intellectual among them; Ravi, a schoolteacher; Gita, a tiny ball of fire; Neena, a heavy-footed Bharatnatyam exponent; Nellie, daughter of a nurse; Chameli, who was in charge of make-up (she worked in a local beauty saloon); Rajiv, who served in the bar and was also our prompter; and a host of others, some of whom would sing and dance before and after our one-act play.

The performance was well attended, Ravi having rounded up a number of students from the local schools; and the lights were working, although we had to cover all doors, windows and exits with blankets to maintain the regulatory black-out. But the stage was old and rickety and things began to go wrong during Neena's dance number when, after a dazzling pirouette, she began stamping her feet and promptly went through the floorboards. Well, to be precise, her lower half went through, while the rest of her remained above board and visible to the audience.

The schoolboys cheered, the curtain came down and we rescued Neena, who had to be sent to the civil hospital with a sprained ankle, Mussoorie's only civilian war casualty.

There was a hold-up, but before the audience could get too restless the curtain went up on our play, a tea-party scene, which opened with Guttoo pouring tea for everyone. Unfortunately, our stage manager had forgotten to put any tea in the pot and poor Guttoo looked terribly put out as he went from cup to cup, pouring invisible tea. 'Damn. What happened to the tea?' muttered Guttoo, a line, which was not in the script. 'Never mind,' said Gita, playing opposite him and keeping her cool. 'I prefer my milk without tea,' and proceeded to pour herself a cup of milk.

After this, everyone began to fluff their lines and our prompter had a busy time. Unfortunately, he'd helped himself to a couple of rums at the bar, so that, whenever one of the actors faltered, he'd call out the correct words in a stentorian voice which could be heard all over the hall. Soon there was more prompting than acting and the audience began joining in with dialogue of their own.

Finally, to my great relief, the curtain came down—to thunderous applause. It went up again, and the cast stepped forward to take a bow. Our prompter, who was also curtain-puller, released the ropes prematurely and the curtain came down with a rush, one of the sandbags hitting poor Guttoo on the head. He has never fully recovered from the blow.

The lights, which had been behaving all evening, now failed us, and we had a real black-out. In the midst of this confusion, someone—it must have been a girl, judging from the overpowering scent of jasmine that clung to her—put her arms around me and kissed me.

When the light came on again, she had vanished.

Who had kissed me in the dark?

As no one came forward to admit to the deed, I could only make wild guesses. But it had been a very sweet kiss, and I would have been only too happy to return it had I known its ownership. I could hardly go up to each of the girls and kiss them in the hope of reciprocation. After all, it might even have been someone from the audience.

Anyway, our concert did raise a few hundred rupees for the war effort. By the time we sent the money to the right authorities, the war was over. Hopefully they saw to it that the money was put to good use.

We went our various ways and although the kiss lingered in my mind, it gradually became a distant, fading memory and as the years passed it went out of my head altogether. Until the other day, almost forty years later...

'Phone for you,' announced Gautam, my seven-year-old secretary.

'Boy or girl? Man or woman?'

'Don't know. Deep voice like my teacher but it says you know her.'

'Ask her name.'

Gautam asked.

'She's Nellie, and she's speaking from Bareilly.'

'Nellie from Bareilly?' I was intrigued. I took the phone, 'Hello,' I said. 'I'm Bonda from Golconda.'

'Then you must be wealthy now.' Her voice was certainly husky. 'But don't you remember me? Nellie? I acted in that play of yours, up in Mussoorie a long time ago.'

'Of course, I remember now.' I was remembering. 'You had a small part, the maidservant I think. You were very pretty. You had dark, sultry eyes. But what made you ring me after all these years.'

'Well, I was thinking of you. I've often thought about you. You were much older than me, but I liked you. After that show, when the lights went out, I came up to you and kissed you. And then I ran away.'

'So it was you! I've often wondered. But why did you run away? I would have returned the kiss. More than once.'

'I was very nervous. I thought you'd be angry.'

'Well, I suppose it's too late now. You must be happily married with lots of children.'

'Husband left me. Children grew up, went away.'

'It must be lonely for you.'

'I have lots of dogs.'

'How many?'

'About thirty.'

'Thirty dogs! Do you run a kennel club?'

'No, they are all strays. I run a dog shelter.'

'Well, that's very good of you. Very humane.'

'You must come and see it sometime. Come to Bareilly. Stay with me. You like dogs, don't you?'

'Er—yes, of course. Man's best friend, the dog. But thirty is a lot of dogs to have about the house.'

'I have lots of space.'

'I'm sure...well, Nellie, if ever I'm in Bareilly, I'll come to see you. And I'm glad you phoned and cleared up the mystery. It was a lovely kiss and I'll always remember it.'

We said our goodbyes and I promised to visit her some day. A trip to Bareilly to return a kiss might seem a bit far-fetched, but I've done sillier things in my life. It's those dogs that worry me. I can imagine them snapping at my heels as I attempt to approach their mistress. Dogs can be very possessive.

'Who was that on the phone?' asked Gautam, breaking in on my reverie.

'Just an old friend.'

'Dada's old girlfriend. Are you going to see her?'

'I'll think about it.'

And I'm still thinking about it and about those dogs. But bliss it was to be in Mussoorie forty years ago, when Nellie kissed me in the dark.

Some memories are best left untouched.

23

A FROG SCREAMS

Sitting near a mountain stream,
I heard a sound like the creaking
Of a branch in the wind,
It was a frog screaming
In the jaws of a long green snake.

I couldn't bear its hideous cry:
Taking two sharp sticks, I made
The twisting snake disgorge the frog,
Who hopped quite cheerfully out of the snake's mouth
And sailed away on a floating log!

Pleased with the outcome,
I released the green grass-snake,

Stood back and wondered:
'Is this what it feels like to be God?'

'Only what it feels like to be English,'
Said God (speaking for a change in French),
'I would have let the snake finish his lunch.'

24

ALL YOU NEED IS PAPER

'Writing is very easy. All you have to do is sit in front of the typewriter until little drops of blood appear on your forehead.'

These immortal words of Red Smith, a forgotten freelance writer, sum up the agony and the ecstasy of those who have made writing their profession.

And it's one reason why I prefer pen and paper to typewriter or computer. A machine in front of me is rather daunting. A pen is more personal and that gives me some control over it—a feeling of power as the words flow with the electric thrill that runs down my arm, through my fingers and onto the clean white page. It is a sensuous act, writing by hand. The feel of the paper, as my hand glides over it, its touch, and its texture. The flow of ink, the gliding motion of the pen, the letters themselves as they appear as if by magic in my individual script. No two people have the same handwriting. Your character, your personality is revealed the minute you put pen to paper.

I'm a compulsive writer of course, and I'll write with whatever is handy. Even crayons will do.

The other night I woke up at about two in the morning, having had a vivid dream about discovering a town where the sun never penetrated, the valley being so deep and precipitous; and yet, apparently, people lived there. There was even a bus service bringing in tourists who wanted to look at the town where people lived in a perpetual shadow. In the dream I left, or rather woke up, before it could get too depressing. But I wanted to remember the dream, as I thought it had the makings of a good story, so I switched on the night light and groped around for a pen or pencil. Both were missing, having been commandeered by Siddharth, Shrishti and Gautam the previous evening. Two in the morning is no time for typing, so I looked around for other means of notation and found Gautam's box of coloured crayons lying on my desk.

I selected a bright orange crayon—a psychological choice, as I wished to disperse the gloom of that sunless town—and made my notes on the back of a large envelope. This is one page of notes that I won't misplace, it stands out so vividly; and some day I might even write the story.

I should use crayons more often!

Desperate writers like me will seize upon any bit of writing material when in need. And I recall that my first literary production was inscribed on sheets of toilet paper.

I was at Prep School in Shimla, and in those days boarders were provided not with rolls of toilet paper but with flat packets of tissue. As there was a wartime paper shortage, boys would often use these bits of tissue for writing letters, doing rough work, or simply making paper aeroplanes. There were no spare exercise books.

Feeling the urge to write a detective story (inspired by a film about the Brighton Strangler), I used up an entire packet of toilet paper in penning my masterpiece. In my story, the mysterious strangler got a job as games' master in our school and went about eliminating all the teachers we disliked. He met his match in the food matron who sprinkled rat poison on his cornflakes.

Unfortunately, one of my friends was overcome by the call of nature. He grabbed my sheets of manuscript and rushed to the toilet, bolting the door, and a little later, when I heard the flush in action, I knew that my story would not reach a publisher.

There have been other lost stories over the years. I don't think any of them have been a great loss to literature, but for personal reasons I would have liked to preserve one or two of them. Like the one about the tikkee-eating contest behind Dehradun's clock tower back in 1956. I wasn't just a spectator, I was a participant, and came a close second having consumed twenty-six fried potato tikkees to Sahib Singh's thirty-two. Sahib was a young Sikh friend who went to England a few years later and did much to popularise samosas, tikkees and chaat in the UK, making a fortune in the process.

I wrote a story about the contest and published it in *The Tribune*, which appeared from Ambala in those far-off days; Chandigarh was only just coming into existence. A clipping of the story went into my scrapbook, but that particular scrapbook was lost when I moved to Delhi and with it several of my early stories. *The Great Tikkee-Eating Contest* was not one of my more memorable works, but it was fun writing it.

As Gautam says, with inexorable logic, 'You can always write it again!'

That is, if it's worth the effort...

Another runaway story was *The Runway Bus*, which appeared in *Sport and Pastime* at about the same time. A bus driver in the metropolis spots his wife riding pillion on a scooter with a stranger, and gives chase, heedless of the convenience of his passengers. He catches up with them near the Qutub Minar, only to find that he has been chasing his wife's double. The bus passengers beat him up.

Then there was *Gone Fishing*, in which the narrator (me) meets a village boy and promises to go fishing with him the next day. But he has to leave town suddenly to take up a job in the Capital. As his train passes over a small bridge, he catches a glimpse of the boy sitting on the banks of a stream, rod and line in hand, fishing by himself. The narrator feels that he has missed something—something more than just a day's fishing—and knows that happiness can be as elusive as a small fish darting away in a mountain stream.

That's a story that I might like to write again.

The invention of the Xerox copying machine meant that I could make as many copies as I wished and the days of lost clippings and typescripts were (almost) over. In my early freelancing days, when I had to use a typewriter, you could take a couple of carbon copies but you could hardly submit these to publishers. Of course, in those days publishers took the trouble to return unwanted manuscripts, so you did not always lose your fair copy. Like most writers, I collected my fair share of rejection slips. Some editors were kind enough to make helpful comments such as 'try again' or 'shows promise', and thus encouraged I would bombard them with articles, stories and poems.

Most publications paid the writer for his work if it was accepted. The sums may have been small but they came in on time. This is not the case today; many successful publications will avoid making payments if they can get away with it.

Many of my rejects (written when I was in my teens) would end up in the pages of a little magazine called *My Magazine of India*, published from Chennai (then called Madras). They would send me a five-rupee money order for every item published. I looked forward to these money orders. With five rupees I could see three films or buy a couple of paperbacks or indulge in a bottle of beer.

If a writer is any good he should expect to be paid for his work. Those who go to vanity publishers and pay to have their books published are doomed to disappointment; they will end up forcing their books upon their unfortunate friends, who will wish they could have had something better for Christmas.

'I have brought you a present!' boomed a retired Brigadier-General the other day, shaking me vigorously by the hand.

'Ah,' I thought, 'perhaps he's brought me a bottle of whisky.' And aloud: 'Do sit down, sir. It's so kind of you to drop in.' And with a flourish he produced two volumes of his memories, all done up in handloom cloth, and with a frontispiece showing the General with a tremendous moustache which would have scared the wits out of me twenty years ago. He still scares the wits out of me, although the moustache has lost much of its early elasticity.

The books are presented to me with a flourish, with a request, or rather order, that I have them reviewed in *Outlook*, *India Today* and the *New York Times*. I promise to do my best and place the books reverently in the most prominent place in my sitting room. As soon as he leaves, I take them down and put them out of sight; they will make good door-stops. But he is too crafty this old General. Suddenly he is back in the room.

'I forgot to autograph them for you,' he says, taking out his fountain pen.

For a few seconds I am at a loss. Then little Gautam appears in the doorway.

'Gautam!' I scold. 'Why did you take those books down from the shelf?' and I retrieve them quickly and hold them out for his autograph. Perhaps his signature will be worth something.

Now I can't use his books as door-stops. He is bound to pop in again, expecting to see them prominently displayed.

A strange thing is human vanity. We all succumb to it from time to time.

I was pleased when the boy from the ration-shop asked me for one of my books. At last, a reader! I presented him with a large format children's book. Lots of pages, good strong paper.

Two or three days later, when I was passing his shop, I noticed a pile of paper bags on the counter. They had all been made from the pages of my book! The boy's father was even then filling one of the bags with channa for one of his customers.

'And what do you require, sir?' he asked me.

'Two rupees worth of peanuts,' I said.

He filled a bag with peanuts and handed them to me. Humbly, I walked away with two pages of my book neatly pasted together to hold peanuts.

I gave the peanuts to Gautam and told him what had happened to the book.

He was quite philosophical about it.

'I suppose the world needs peanuts more than it needs books,' he said.

I couldn't argue with that. Gautam's worldly wisdom and advice is always on a par with Mr Dick's in *David Copperfield*.

We strolled into the sitting room and I surveyed my shelves of books. The General's memoirs immediately caught my eye. I took the two large volumes down from the shelf. Gautam noticed the wicked glint in my eyes.

'What are you going to do?' he asked.

'Come,' I said. 'We are going to make paper bags.'

25

SONG FOR A BEETLE IN A GOLDFISH BOWL

A beetle fell into the goldfish bowl,
Hey-ho!
The beetle began to struggle and roll,
Ho-hum!
The window was open, the moon shone bright,
The crickets were singing with all their might,
But a blundering beetle had muddled his flight
And here he was now, in a watery plight,
Having given the goldfish a terrible fright,
Ho-hum, hey-ho!

The beetle swam left, the beetle swam right,

Hum-ho!
Along came myself—I said, 'Lord, what a sight!
That poor old beetle will drown tonight.
Ho-hum.
A beetle is just an insect, I hear,
But what if I fell in a vat full of beer?
I'd be brewed to light lager if no one came near—
(It happened I'm told, to a man in Tangier)—
Ho-hum, ho-hum.'

With my finger and thumb
The beetle I seized,
The goldfish looked pleased,
The window was open, the moon shone bright,
I thrust the beetle far out in the night,
And he bumbled away in a staggering flight,
Ho-hum, hey-ho,
Good night!

26

ODDS AND ENDS

'Laugh and be fat, sir.'
Ben Jonson

★

'Light suppers make long lives.'
Granny

★

'Don't let your tongue cut your throat.'
Granny

★

'If you don't have courage, have strong legs.'
Uncle Ken

★

Avoid long speeches. The less a man knows, the longer he takes to tell it.

★

Try loving your enemies. If nothing else, you'll confuse them.

★

Adventure is when a child crawls across the floor, grabs the leg of a chair, and stands up for the first time.

★

'If you cannot win, make the fellow ahead of you exert himself to the utmost!'

Uncle Ken

★

'You will sometimes be punished when you do not deserve it. Before giving vent to your indignation, reflect on how often you have deserved punishment without receiving it.'

Anon

★

They always come so quickly—those turning points in life—and always down a lane we are not watching.

★

'God gave us our faces. We gave ourselves our expressions.'

Granny

★

Bad times are good times to prepare for better times.

★

Gautam is always polite. One day a visitor who had a very large nose came to see us. We told Gautam not to say anything about his enormous nose. The visitor arrived, Gautam stared at him, smiled, and then turning to me, said, 'Dada, what a pretty little nose he has!'

★

'Be sparing of speech, and things will come right of themselves.'

Lao-Tsze

★

'Honour thy food, receive it thankfully, eat it contentedly, never hold it in contempt.'

Manu

★

'There is skill in all things, even in scrambling an egg.'

Granny

★

The electricity bill has been going up ever since I started telling the children ghost stories at night. Siddharth, Shrishti and Gautam insist on sleeping with all the lights on. This results in moths flying in through the open windows.
The other night I swallowed a moth.
'What did it taste like?' asked Gautam.
'Chocolate,' I said.
He doesn't believe me.

'Step out lightly, step out brightly, and luck will come your way.'
Uncle Ken

'A merry heart does more good than any medicine.'
Granny

Chart your own course through life. What the stars foretell is strictly for astrologers.